Underworld Life . . . Complete

Oakland Tribune

"I can't pay you again, tonight. I haven't any money on me."

"Baby, you ain't had no bread for two weeks now. So, what're we going to do? I got to live too, you know."

"I'll get on my feet soon, I'll pay you back for everything in a week or so."

"Maggie, I'm lonely tonight. That empty room's getting on my nerves."

"Yeah? You want me to come home with you?"

SENSATIONAL . . . ABSORBING
Indianapolis Times

Judge John M. Murtagh, Chief Justice
Court of Special Sessions, New York City

and Sara Harris

WHO LIVE IN SHADOW

WILDSIDE PRESS

To Mary and Arnold

BOOK I

Junktown,
U. S. A.

Chapter **1 Long and Lonely Nights**

It has been a long and lonely night around 116th Street in East Harlem. Now, it is 2 A.M. The morning is dismal and gray. It is cold. Still, there are people walking up and down the block. Trying to keep warm, some of them huddle in the doorways of the dreary tenements and the closed-up shops. They look sick and strained and they behave like conspirators.

They are conspirators. They are here in East Harlem—Junktown, U.S.A., the world's capital of the drug trade—to buy narcotics. They know that they are operating against the law and that the men who share their doorways may be detectives who will place them under arrest as soon as they make their purchases.

"But a junkie* can't worry about getting busted by the coppers. Not when she's getting down and starting to feel sick. Listen, when you've been hooked as long as I have, thirty-two years come next week, you can die if you don't get your junk when you need it." Mary Jane Morris, sixty-two years old, speaks these words. It is said along the street that she had important friends before she became demented out of her need for heroin. Today, however, she associates only with other addicts, people like Hubert, a pallid, scrawny youth, who is lurking in a doorway with her now. Hubert's

* For definitions of addict and underworld terms used in text, see the Glossary.

7

mother died last year, and because he misses her so much, he likes to pretend that Mary Jane is his mother.

Mrs. Morris and Hubert have the same connection. George McCrae, a most successful pusher, is a brassy, snorting boy of eighteen who is not himself smitten with the need for narcotics. He is scornful of his customers. He calls them "goofs." His contempt, of course, does not prevent him from making deals and from hanging endlessly onto every well-fixed person he can persuade to buy from him. It is the money he gets from the goofs, after all, that enables him to live as well as he does.

This morning George McCrae is late. He promised to be on the corner of 116th Street and Second Avenue at one o'clock sharp. And here it is an hour later and no George. Mrs. Morris and Hubert are desperate with the cold and the anxiety. Maybe George has decided to give them up. What can they do if he doesn't come? Give a stranger the eye? It's a possibility. Addicts and connections can often sniff each other out. They share recognizable high signs. But many addicts still get into trouble while they are trying to find new sellers.

"Cat, do *you* glim what happened to George?" The junkie jive is humorous in the mouth of Mrs. Morris. Doubtless, outsiders would chuckle to hear her. But they don't know the life and language of East 116th Street. When you're in the gutter, Mrs. Morris often thinks to herself, you have to do as the gutter-rats do.

Hubert grimaces. "No. Maybe he dropped dead or something."

"God forbid."

"Like, dig, chick, if he dropped dead, I would too."

A sixty-two-year-old woman from the other side of the tracks and Hubert calls her "chick." Such is the etiquette in this morass. Who, here, is iconoclast enough to buck it?

At last George McCrae arrives. He is cautious and pretends that he does not know his customers. He walks carelessly into a tenement in the middle of the block. Any watching police officer might think he lived there and was returning home from a late date. Mrs. Morris and Hubert, fevered and greedy, want to dart after him but they don't dare. They are not so addleheaded. George will never sell to them again if they permit their frenzy to show.

So they wait as patiently as they can. Five minutes. Ten minutes. George comes out after fifteen minutes. Mrs. Morris and Hubert wait another fifteen minutes and then, half-frozen, they stumble into the building George has left. They look into a crevice behind the stairs. Thank God, the stuff is there as always. Now that she actually has the heroin in hand, Mrs. Morris smiles tenderly to herself.

"Got to go now," she tells Hubert.

"Yeah," he says, "I'm off too."

Outside the tenement, pretty seventeen-year-old Maggie Smith is waiting for her connection, Sonny. She has a far-away look and walks slowly up and down. But once she spies Sonny she begins running, pushing against the wind.

"Sonny," she says, "I sure did get down, and I mean down, man. I had to wait for you so long."

"Well, I'm here now."

Sonny is in his sixties, a paunchy, gray-haired man with a stale face.

"Sonny?" Maggie speaks softly.

"Mm?"

"I can't pay you again, tonight. I haven't any money on me."

"Baby, you ain't had no bread for two weeks now. So, what're we going to do? I got to live too, you know."

"I'll get on my feet soon, I'll pay you back for everything in a week or so."

"Maggie, I'm lonely tonight. That empty room's getting on my nerves."

"Yeah? You want me to come home with you?"

Maggie had gone to Sonny's room once before. He had made love to her and then he had called her vulgar names and attacked her with his fists. Later he had given her a double shot of heroin. Tonight, Maggie has amnesia for everything except the double shot.

"Come on, Sonny, let's go."

Before Sonny and Maggie have gone off, old Joe comes along the street. He moves slowly, as though his shoes are too heavy for his feet. He is headed toward Benny's shooting gallery.

Benny's is a typical gathering place for narcotics addicts. It could be located in any of a score of large cities in this country. It is a tattered tenement apartment, peeling, splotched, dusty, haunted by addicts who come to buy their heroin and shoot it into themselves in the company of their peers. It is owned and presided over by a sleek, fat peddler known as Benny the Bum.

Benny's is a strange, busy place with people moving in and out all day and night. Now, at four or so in the morning, with its lights dimmed for the sake of economy, not atmosphere, it has settled down to its last load of customers. They are all, as they would say, "coasting, floating in high, racing our motors and all lit up."

Here is Jack, actually forty and looking sixty with his gaunt, hollow face. There is Marge, a cheap streetwalker from her getup and looks. And young Mark, with the thick-lensed spectacles. He may be threadbare, but he's fastidiously clean all the same. Here's J. L., brown-skinned, tall, wearing a natty, flashy, sporty suit that must have been expensive when it was bought. Where did he get the suit? "Oh, from a working chick, you know, a *working* chick. I used to have a whole stable of them, boy." And there's Chinky. Wong. No racial or national lines are ever drawn at Benny the Bum's.

To look at them, not just Jack and J. L. and Chinky, but all Benny's customers, maybe ten or twelve sickly, skinny, slovenly-appearing people, you would never guess how they were seeing themselves this morning. And they wouldn't tell you. They don't care to talk or to mix today. All they want is to be left alone to their laughing and their scratching. Most of them sit slumped in their chairs, more than half asleep, on the goof, on the nod. A couple mutter and twitch. Some stare straight ahead, remote, cold, stoned out of this world. It's where they want to be. They are not fond of the workaday world, the everyday world of reality.

And now here comes old Joe. Once he was a Benny habitué too and he knows the secret of gaining entrance to the place—three short rings and two long ones. Benny opens the door.

"Oh, it's you."

"Yeah, Benny, can I come in?"

"I guess."

Most of Benny's customers are lost in their private worlds. But a few look up and see Joe.

"Jeez, Benny, what're you running here anyways, a shooting gallery or a morgue? What the hell you want to let *Joe* in for?"

It is strange to hear addicts so critical. Usually, when they are sitting together as they are here at Benny's, there's a kind of peculiar fraternity among them. Not the kind that would cause them to look out for one another—they can't afford that luxury—but still the kind that keeps them from backing off from other people, from glaring down their noses at them. Joe is a different story. He stands by himself, lonely and obsessed. He is what is known around Junktown as a birdcage hype, a flophouse type, a boot-and-shoer, a lame, lazy, crazy cat. For some odd reason, bad luck dogs him, and not only him, but everyone he knows. He is one man sure to attract all the gazers, all the whiskers and uncles, all the narcotics agents who are on the make today. Or if not the gazers and the whiskers and uncles, then the long-tailed rats, the no-good stools, who'll be on his tail and report him to the gazers. Then the gazers will raid whatever shooting gallery he happens to be patronizing. Everyone will be in trouble.

Everybody is giving Joe the evil eye. "Stay away from *my* door, cat; I got nothing for you." But Joe goes up to them anyway, one by one. He can't help himself. He's got an oil-burning habit and no money with which to buy heroin.

"Listen, man, I ain't scored my connection. Give me a little today and I'll return your favor tomorrow."

"Blow."

"Hell, cat, the monkey on my back's getting bigger every minute."

"I got a monkey of my own."

"Give me a break."

"A break? Tell you what you do, man, like you shot it in? Now sneeze it out."

"I'll drop dead, I bet you."

"What kind of flowers you want at the funeral?"

Finally he puts the bite on Benny himself. He stands in front of him, shabby and mournful.

"Benny, I got to have some stuff."

"What do you want I should do, give you some, feed you like you was my little kitty or something?"

All of a sudden, Joe drops his whining tone. "Benny, I'm no stoolie. But if I can't score from you I can from the coppers. You tell them a thing or two, they're glad to turn you on."

Benny has no choice but to give Joe his heroin. He has been catering to such small-time leeches all his life in the business. He knows there is no honor among them, no loyalty.

Joe is throwing out no idle threat. Either Benny fixes him up or he talks to the narcotics agents.

"One thing, though;" Benny says, "rats like Joe are not so expensive to keep off your tail as the coppers are. They come around to your place and tell you 'Gimme.' You better not argue with them, either. The payoffs some of those coppers rake in! You ought to hear them yell 'Gimme.' They don't whine or cry. They just say 'Gimme.' Junkies make a slow-motion killing on your pocketbook. Uncles do it in a big way. 'It just happens we're out of funds tonight. All we want from you is a couple of hundred, Benny. Just a loan, you know, Benny.' "

Benny used to think when he first started in the business that he would get to be an important man someday. Then he could stop making the little payoffs. He'd envisioned his place as a hangout for all the biggest narcotics men in town. He'd thought his connection would keep leading him on to bigger and better connections until finally he would become friendly with the biggest ones of all.

It never happened that way. Benny's connection was only a step or two above him in the hierarchy and couldn't have introduced him to the right men even if he had wanted to. And it is laughable to think that this place could ever have become a gathering spot. The big men can go where they please, Sardi's, the Blue Angel, the Versailles, the Chambord. "They're great ones for cashmere coats and coupes de villes and Scotch on the rocks, 'with just a hint of lemon peel, please,' " Benny says. "They got gorgeous chicks hanging on their necks. What do they need with me?"

Benny knows about the big men's activities. He has often thought that if he were to tell what he knows he could "blast a couple of coppers out of their easy chairs." He never will tell, though. He wants to go on living.

"Well," he says, "so you lose your mind and you talk a little. And one day you're walking along Second Avenue and you meet a friend who says:·

" 'Hey, Benny, there's a telephone call for you in the candy store.'

"You go to the candy store with your friend. He's no plug-ugly. He's your pal and you go with him. Sure, if you had the brains you were born with you might not trust him. But, hell, you got to trust somebody in this world. So you go into the candy store. The guy who owns it is another pal. He also tells you about the call. Yeah, you wonder why does anyone call me here. Why don't they call me at my own place? But still you trust your friends and you go into the telephone booth.

" 'Yeah,' you say, 'Hello?'

"And there's no one on the other end of the line. So your heart begins beating fast. You know now your friend's been giving you the business. You know you're in a jam. Your legs turn to lead. You can't move them. Then in the split second you allow yourself to hate your friends, a big black Cadillac pulls up to the door of the candy store and two men you never saw before get out. Of course if you had seen them before you wouldn't know it—them with the big flop hats and the long overcoats buttoned up around their necks and hanging down to their ankles. They walk up to the phone booth you're standing in, they pull out their sawed-off shotguns and you've gone out to meet your judgment day. Then, when they've finished you off, they wave goodbye to your friends and they're gone back to Chicago or wherever the hell they come from."

Benny knows what can happen to squealers. He's seen shootings occur. Sometimes a man would be walking along the street and be shot in the back. Benny gets sick and melancholy when he thinks of the gangsters' guns. But then he feels a rallying cry in him—well, why not? Life is a gamble. Drugs mean money and money is what matters and everybody knows there is more money in the drugs all the way up and down the line than in any other business in the world.

Well, take one kilo, 2.2 pounds of heroin that's purchased in Italy or Istanbul or Red China for, say, three thousand dollars. By the time this kilo reaches the customer on the street it has been diluted some twenty times with a drug called mannita which increases its volume, with milk sugar which increases its weight, with quinine which has the same bitter taste as pure heroin and with opium powder which has the same color as heroin. Now the kilo, the same kilo which cost three thousand dollars, brings in about three hundred thousand—increased a hundred times. There is plenty of money for everyone on the selling end of the business, plenty for Benny the Bum as well as for the right men. Why should Benny tell the law anything?

Benny says he'd take a rap before he'd talk to the authorities. He says,

"In my day I did bits in every rinky-dink pen in town. A copper would pick me up and give me the business and I'd give it right back.

" 'All right, Benny, you might as well tell us now as later. Who's your connection?' this copper'd say. I'd say,

" 'Connection? Connection?' Like, listen man, I ain't got no connections. 'I don't know what you're talking about.'

"After a while I got damn fed up with having to give coppers the comedy and I'd go salty on them. I knew I'd land in jail anyhow."

It took several years before Benny the Bum discovered the secret of proper contact with the officers. He began naming them names, but not connections' names, only addicts' names.

"That's right;" he says, "every time they get me I sing them some song. I give them the name of every griefer or shoe-and-booter who hangs out in my joint. That way everybody is happy: the big boys and me, and the coppers and their bosses who can count on good old Benny to keep their goddamn pens filled up for them. Even the junk hogs aren't too bad off. What the hell, they get cured of their habits, don't they? Cured! Well, anyways they can start off cheaper than they been doing before they went to the pen.

"I'm all right," Benny adds. "I'm pretty lucky now that I learned to put down the right psychology. I got myself in like Flynn with the coppers and the big boys too. And what could be sweeter than that?"

And who suffers from Benny's nimble verbiage? Only the addicts. According to Benny the Bum, nobody cares about them except "maybe their mothers or sweethearts or wives."

"Well," he says, "so to hell with the junkies. The junkies are jerks. They're characters. They have no friends. Listen, a junkie can love you like a mother and he'll still sell you out for a shot. You know the difference between a longtailed rat who's a stool pigeon of the lowest order and a mouse who's just a plain stool pigeon? Well, a mouse won't finger his own old lady. That's one of our jokes around here."

Benny's homely opinions of drug addicts are shared by the addicts themselves. To one another they say:

"Better not tell a junkie who you are. He's sure to tell the gazers."

"Better not let junkies know where you live. You'll go home and find they swiped all your stuff away from you."

Drug addicts cannot afford the milk of human kindness. It's a furtive life they lead, one that does not make for loyalty or trustworthiness. They are weak, frightened people. In fact, there is another old joke among them:

"An alky gets drunk and then he goes home and beats up his old lady. A junkie gets loaded and then he goes home and his old lady beats him."

When addicts let themselves go, most of them talk in wails.

"I feel like I been in the okey-doke," one says. "You know, like I spent my whole life behind bars."

In one way or another, all addicts conceive of themselves in jail. Their hard feelings go back to their early childhoods.

"My old lady. She's good-natured. She's got a big heart. Hell, she only hit me on the head with a shoe a couple times. My old man used to hold my hand over the fire."

"I was an orphan. Nobody wants you if you don't really belong to them. I was put in twelve foster homes. The mothers always said, 'We don't want this kid no more. Hell, he bites his fingernails, wets the bed.' Out of the whole foster mothers, I made one. She dug me and I dug her. But wouldn't you know she'd up and die on me? I threw myself in her coffin. They pulled me out again."

"I'm in prison now. All right, it's no worse than the prison I spent my childhood in. I hated my stepmother so much, my sister and I tried to put poison in her oatmeal one day."

And so, most addicts, carrying their childhood along with

the monkeys on their backs, have tried to down their feelings. Junkie jive, mystic and nimble, full of fantasy, is one indication of their personality problems. Narcotics addicts are never, as the rest of us are at times, lonely, hurt, miserable, depressed. They get "brung down." They just "flip their lids." Similarly, few addicts will ever say, "Darling, I love you." The best they can manage is, "Baby, I dig you. You're the greatest."

You can ask an addict, "Why—how come you can't say 'I love you.' " He will usually answer: "Them words ain't cool. They just ain't cool enough."

And there, in a few words, you have an important tenet of the addict philosophy—"Cool it, don't give yourself away. Don't let on you want Mama, Papa, anyone. You let people know you need them and they'll put the shackles on you."

Addicts are full of rage and guilt and self-pity when they're sober. But they say that once they get high all those feelings change. They're not tense any more. They go quiet inside. They don't curse or fight. They forget about all the mistakes they made. They forget how it was when they were little half-pint kids, "knocking myself out and nobody gave a damn." They forget how they always kept their noses buried because they thought they were low and they didn't want anyone else to know it. They even forget what a crying need they had to love and to be loved. They forget they've always blamed themselves because nobody seemed to care about them.

There is one small notion, one small idea a person who is not an addict himself can have of the groping and contortions that go on in the addict's soul. You get the notion when you watch what they call "going on the boot." That is when they leave the needle in their arms after all the drug has been absorbed. They twitch the needle until the blood comes and most of them smile with the pain. It is a terrifying sight. You want to ask them: "Why are you treating yourself this way? What have you done that is so terrible? You haven't killed anybody, have you? What do you want to go and kill *yourself* for?"

It's a little death in a way, getting high on horse. It's kissing real life goodbye. Narcotics addicts like playing dead. They need a fast relief from life. They say, "If you know how to use the needle you get a lift the quick way. You can get high as Pike's Peak when you know how to use the needle. And you know what, you can curl up sugarsweet and dreamy like you were a little baby. No worries. No troubles. Like you were a little baby or like you were dead and gone out of this crazy, mixed-up world."

Many of today's addicts are young—fifteen, sixteen, seventeen years old. They all say that they do not know one moment of genuine peace or happiness. Intervals of elation, or exhilaration, yes. But, even while they are "under the influence," they are aware of the fact that drugs can bring them only illusions. They say they can foresee their futures, the loss of health and hope and self-respect. They talk about other addicts, older ones, who died in prisons and mental institutions. They tell of addicts who are gutter-bums in streets and flophouses.

Why then do they become addicts? You hear a lot today about the hip younger generation taking narcotics for the kicks. Nothing could be farther from the truth. Young addicts are not seeking kicks. They are exploring new ways for dealing with their buried pains.

Teen-agers must always grapple with life. Adolescence is at best a period of considerable insecurity and social adjustment. And not just for slum children. Children from respectable, harmonious families can also be seething inside and trying to find means for making themselves more comfortable. Perhaps parents, in addition to worrying about the peddlers who hang around the schools, ought also to begin thinking about how they may be failing their offspring. Certainly children who have been taught how to solve their own problems, how to meet their difficulties and disappointments, will not become addicts—not matter how many pushers they run into.

Marilyn Green was never taught to solve her problems or meet her disappointments. And when she reached her adolescence she was a frightened and despondent girl. But you'd never know it to look at her. She is a pretty girl, blonde, blue-eyed, long-legged. Her father is an accountant in Evanston, Illinois. Her mother was a schoolteacher before she married. Despite some friction between the parents, the three of them—Marilyn, her father and her mother—always lived a close-knit family life until Marilyn was fifteen. That was the year she acquired her first real girl-friend. She had always been a shy girl who had found it hard to come close to children of her own age. Perhaps she was too attached to her parents. Perhaps she was too studious. Or maybe there was not enough flicker and frolic in her. At any rate, in the old days she had no friends. And then Jane O'Rourke came into her life. Jane lived on the other side of the tracks. Her family was poor. And Marilyn's mother and father did not approve of her.

Marilyn's parents did not understand that Jane was a tonic to Marilyn, a shot in the arm, a first love. She was the opposite of Marilyn, eager and high-spirited. She was full of lunacy, so that there were times when Marilyn laughed wildly with her. She was dark-haired and attractive, and she liked to wear tight sweaters and jeans. Marilyn thought she had a wonderful figure. But Marilyn's mother said Jane looked like a baby cooch-dancer.

Marilyn was troubled when her parents maligned Jane. She fought with them. Then she felt guilty about the fights. She thought it was due to her badness that the once-peaceful home was turning into a battleground. But she could not permit her parents to ridicule her best friend. All the miserable quarrels she had with them came down to one thing: to Marilyn, friendship was a romantic miracle. But how could a bumbling girl explain such a thought? Marilyn wanted to imitate Jane in every way. Jane wore make-up and so Marilyn fought with her parents about wearing lipstick.

"I declare," her mother said, "no daughter of mine's going to get done up like a circus clown."

"I'm not done up like a circus clown."

"Well, you're too young to be wearing make-up."

"I'm not too young. All the girls wear lipstick."

"Not nice girls. Only girls like Jane and the rest of that crowd she travels with."

"Don't pick on my friends, Mother."

"I don't like your tone, young lady."

"And I don't like you making me look ridiculous with my crowd."

"Oh, so it's your crowd now. I thought it was Jane O'Rourke's crowd."

Well, Jane's crowd was also Marilyn's, and why didn't her mother understand how much it meant to a girl to have a crowd of her own? Marilyn hated to talk back to her mother, but her mother irritated her so there was nothing else to do. "What is this with parents?" Marilyn used to think to herself. "All your life they think you're wonderful and then, as soon as you start growing up, they begin disapproving of you."

"Those girls Jane's got you running with are cheap, Marilyn."

Marilyn said, "Why, because they wear lipstick? Because their parents aren't trying to make babies out of them? On account of you, all the kids are going to think I'm queer."

Her father said, "That's enough of that kind of talk, my girl. You'll wear lipstick when your mother says you're ready, and not one day sooner."

Marilyn thought that if her father and mother didn't understand her need to fit in with the other girls she couldn't make them. But she didn't have to yield to their pressures. She could buy herself a lipstick and wear it behind their backs. She justified her duplicity by telling herself that what they didn't know wouldn't hurt them.

But even after the lipstick problem was solved, home was still more or less an arsenal to Marilyn, and life there was still an unending contest between her and her parents.

"Who ever heard of a nice girl wearing blue jeans all the time?" the mother asked.

Marilyn gave her usual answer: "All the girls wear them."

"What girls?"

"My friends."

"Friends!"

Marilyn's jeans were too figure-hugging for her father's taste, too. He said, "They're revolting. And, while we're talking, I want to tell you something else—this new hip-swinging you call walking has got to stop. Who do you think you are, Marilyn Monroe?"

"Daddy, all the girls walk the way I do."

"Well, you're not all the girls. You're my daughter and I won't have you making a show of yourself."

Her father's attack on her walk was an attack on Marilyn's dream-self. During the hours she had practiced that walk in front of the mirror, she had thought of herself as Marilyn Monroe.

"Very sexy," she had told herself in the stylish Hollywood voice she was also cultivating. "Very, very sexy."

Marilyn thought a lot about sex. She and Jane and the other girls talked a good deal about it. Most of the girls were dating and were full of scandal about the boys with whom they went. Marilyn, who was still forbidden dates, listened avidly to the others. She could not get enough of their conversation. She was like a Peeping Tom flitting from one keyhole to another.

"Well," Jane said, "Howard wanted me to go all the way. I said, 'When I get married, man, when I get married.'"

Another girl said, "You know you got to expect a boy to ask you to go all the way if you pet with him. Me, I'll only neck."

"I'll pet," Jane said, "if I feel like it. And I'll stop when I feel like it."

"You get boys excited that way."

"So what? If they don't like it they don't need to date me again."

Marilyn had her first date when she was sixteen. He was a boy named Denny, whom she had met through Jane. He was good-looking, tall, dark and sharply dressed. He was eighteen and drove a Chevrolet convertible. He lived in Chicago, only a short drive from Marilyn's home.

For days before her date, Marilyn was caught up in a dizzy whirl. Would she be equal to a sophisticate like Denny? Would she know how to behave with him?

Jane said, "You musn't let him go too far on your first date. A good-night kiss and maybe a little necking."

"But will he ask me out again if that's all I do?"

"Well, baby, you got to take that chance."

It was all right for Jane to talk about taking chances. The boys all followed her around. Jane knew how to handle her men. She tried to impart some of her knowledge to Marilyn.

"Make promises with your eyes. A boy'll take a lot of hammy clowning if he thinks there's something in it for later."

But Marilyn couldn't be a hammy clown. There was too much desperation in her. She felt herself too insignificant. She was too afraid of being seen through. And after she had spent the long evening with Denny, she could not clown with him for another, more important reason. She found herself caught up in something she had not reckoned with. Certainly, while she and Denny sat in his parked car, she remembered what Jane had told her about how far to permit him to go—"a good-night kiss or two, and maybe let him hold his face against yours for a while."

But Marilyn herself couldn't stop with a kiss. She felt she had fallen in love with Denny and wanted him as much as he wanted her. No one had ever talked about love to Marilyn. Her mother and father would have been ashamed of such a conversation and her girl-friends were only concerned with sex. They were worried about rules and regulations. Why didn't Jane and the others know how sweet a boy's embrace could be? Why hadn't anyone told Marilyn that a boy's kiss could make a girl throb with pleasure? Marilyn had never before felt the way she did with Denny. There was something great and wonderful about surrendering herself to him.

In the morning, of course, she was revolted by what she had done. She felt like an animal or an ogre. Jane could control her feelings but she, Marilyn, must be oversexed. A boy made a pass at her and she lost herself completely. Sure, take me, here I am. She was easy game in spite of all her mother and father had taught her.

"I don't know how I got through those next days after my date with Denny," Marilyn tells. "I just drooped around the house. He called a couple of times but I wouldn't see him. And yet I was thrilled just to hear him talk. He called me 'baby' and I almost collapsed. He kept calling me, too. He was persistent. I guess you could say he pursued me. He'd wait outside of school for me. I'd say, 'why do you keep coming around like this? He'd say it was because he loved me.

"Well, I went out with him. I couldn't help myself. He used to make little passes at me but he never tried to go all the way again. I found out later why that was. He was on the junk, and junkies don't have too much yen for sex. But I didn't know that then. I was just so in love with Denny I couldn't see straight. I made it my business to stick with him as much as possible."

One night, after Marilyn had been seeing Denny for four months, he started her smoking marijuana. It happened on a night when Jane was out with them.

"Come on, kids," he said. "Let's light up a couple of weeds for kicks."

Marilyn didn't want to smoke but she didn't know how to say no to Denny. Besides, Jane was eager to try the marijuana. The first time they smoked, both Marilyn and Jane were sick. But the second time was different.

"I don't know how to describe those first kicks," Marilyn says today. "Well, it's like you're out of this world. Your head's buzzing but it doesn't matter. I felt so easy inside after I'd lighted up. Everything seemed funny to me. You know, somebody said something and I'd burst out laughing. Or I'd just sit around giggling for no reason. I forgot all about everything, and I guess that's what I was out to do."

Once she'd tried the marijuana, it wasn't difficult to take the next step to heroin. She could not resist the stories she heard about its effects. Marylin was hooked two weeks after Denny gave her her first shot of heroin. "The horse didn't give me the thrill I'd gotten out of my first weed," she explains. "You get a different feeling from horse. You stop worrying about anything. Like I didn't worry any more about how badly I'd treated my parents. Or about whether Denny really loved me."

Denny supplied Marilyn with heroin for three months. During that time, she met him once or twice every day. And she lived for those times. Whenever she was home she was restless. She couldn't relax. It seemed she couldn't read a book or watch television without squirming. She couldn't eat her meals and she seemed to grow thinner every day. Her mother tried to get her to go to a doctor, but Marilyn became angry every time the suggestion was made. Her school grades, which had always been so good, went steadily downward. She wouldn't discuss any reasons with her parents. She'd give them a twisted, bitter smile when they asked her what was wrong.

Despite the changes in her personality, Marilyn's parents did not realize she was addicted until the night Denny refused to supply her with more heroin.

"I got to scrounge to get my own stuff," he said. "I been taking care of you long enough."

"What'll I do then?"

"Get the money from your old man."

"I couldn't do that."

"Well then, you got to find another way. You could go with customers I get you. I know plenty fellows could get smitten by a kitten like you."

Marilyn was horrified. She told Denny she never wanted to see him again. And she also said she was going off heroin.

Denny laughed in her face.

Later that night she discovered the reason for his laughter. She woke up writhing, every muscle in torment. She couldn't breathe. She felt dizzy. She began sobbing out loud. Her parents ran into her room. Between gasping, tortured breaths, she told them she was hooked.

"I got to have a shot," she said. Her mother and father couldn't believe her at first. Not their daughter. Marilyn was no uncared-for slum child. How was this possible? They were outraged, and yet, when they looked at Marilyn, they felt a terrible pity for her. The sweat poured down her face and she tried to beat her head against the wall.

Her mother held her head to keep her from beating it and kept muttering "darling" to herself. Her father ran to the phone and called the family doctor.

"Listen," he said, "you've got to come at once. Marilyn's terribly sick." When the doctor arrived, he entered Marilyn's room and talked to her briefly. Mr. Green explained that Marilyn had a narcotics habit and asked whether there was any medication to combat it. When the doctor said no, he begged him to give her a shot to relieve her.

"I'm sorry," the doctor said. "I can't give it to her."

"What do you mean, you can't give it to her? She's miserable."

"I'm sorry. I really am."

"What is all this 'sorry' business? My child's sick. You're a doctor and you've got to help her."

"I can't help her. It's against the law."

"What'll I do, then?"

"Call a hospital. Maybe they'll take her. I doubt that they will. But there's a chance. Anyhow, she won't die."

Gasps and cries shook Marilyn's body. She and her mother both sobbed. The mother prayed through her tears.

Marilyn's father called three hospitals. None of them would admit a drug addict.

"Daddy," Marilyn screamed out, "you got to find Denny. He's got stuff. Tell him I must have some."

All the time the father sought Denny he wrestled with dim thoughts about a law that would not allow a doctor to treat a sick child. He had never seen his daughter so sick. A doctor should be with her now, kind and soft-spoken, offering her human understanding and medical relief. Instead, she and her mother were home alone while he had to beg a boy he hated, a member of the criminal element, to help her out of her misery.

Once he found Denny, Marilyn's father forced himself to speak as though he was unaware of the boy's part in his daughter's tragedy. "Denny, I want to talk to you."

Denny said, "You never wanted to talk to me before. How come you're so anxious now?"

"It's Marilyn. She's . . . hooked."

"You don't say? I could've told you something would happen to her sooner or later. She was too wild for her own good."

"She's sick. She's got to have a shot."

"What do you want me to do?"

Mr. Green turned and suddenly seize Denny by the shoulders. "Denny, you've got to give me what she needs."

"I don't know what you're talking about. What makes you think I got any junk or know where to get it?"

"Please."

Denny's voice was soft. "Get out of here, old man. Leave me alone."

"Denny, you made an addict out of Marilyn."

"You say that again, I'll knock you down. That stuff don't go with me. I'll call the police on you, you make accusations. I'm not afraid of you."

Mr. Green forced himself to control his feelings. "I'm not here to accuse you. I'm here to beg you to help Marilyn."

Finally, Denny gave him a small packet of heroin. "It'll be ten bucks," he said harshly. "And don't come to me any more."

The day after they found out about her addiction, Marilyn's parents conferred with a social worker in the Community Health Center.

"I wish I knew how to advise you," she said. "But in the whole country there are only two hospitals that can handle cases like Marilyn's. They're both overcrowded, naturally. Besides they're part jail. There are armed guards who patrol the premises. There are iron grills on the windows and bars on the doors. If you send Marilyn to one of those hospitals, many of her companions will be federal prisoners, old-timers, prostitutes, thieves, and the like. I have to tell you honestly that Marilyn's likely to be scared out of her wits by what she may experience there. And I don't know how much good the treatment will do her. Of course she'll be off drugs while she is inside but I haven't heard of too many cases of permanent cure. Most people, especially teen-agers, are fine when they're in an institutional setting but once they get out and the pressures start piling up again they generally return to the habit. I hate to say this to you but, due to our lack of decent treatment facilities for addicts, I can't hold out too much hope for Marilyn."

But, because there seemed nothing else to do, Marilyn's parents had her committed to the federal hospital at Lexington, Kentucky.

"At first sight," Marilyn said, "Lexington looked like a country club. The location was lovely. It was on a high hill right in the middle of the Kentucky bluegrass country. You could look out and see racing stables. But of course the bars hit you right away. I got a pain in my stomach when I saw them. I got hysterical. It was terrible to cry so with strangers, and not be able to stop. They took most of the clothes I'd brought from home away from me. Then they searched me all over for junk. It was embarrassing."

On her arrival Marilyn, along with all the other incoming patients, was sent to the "shooting gallery," the withdrawal ward.

"You get methadon when you come in," Marilyn tells, "and it's cut down gradually. It didn't help me much. I was terrible from the minute I got in. I gagged and vomited and had diarrhea. I don't know when I was in worse agony. I think I lost five pounds the first day I was in. I stayed in the shooting gallery about a week. And then they sent me to 'skid row.' I guess you'd call it the convalescent ward. They feed you lots of rich foods and you're supposed to gain your strength back there. After you get through with skid row, they put you in population with the rest of the junkies. That's when the fun begins. Boy, what I didn't learn in population."

She saw at first hand the countless ruses addicts invent for duping the guards and obtaining narcotics. There was Slippery Sal, who made soap imprints of the guards' keys to the narcotics closet and was able to keep her friends supplied with heroin. She liked the young girls and she'd give them shots in return for kisses. And there was young Gregory, a month or so older than Marilyn, who cut his tongue so he could cough up blood. The stories he told were so convincing that the staff often gave him narcotics to "keep him comfortable."

"I used to like to hear about how old Greg put it over on the staff," Marilyn says. "They all thought they were so smart, you know. They used to tell us, 'We're on to all your junkie tricks.' At first it burned me when I heard them talk like that. But after a while I got used to it. I had to admit myself that we junkies were a tricky bunch. I always think of myself as part of 'we junkies' since I've been to Lexington. It's funny. There's us, 'we junkies,' I mean. And there's other people, including the staff in Lexington.

"Actually the staff's not bad. Of course they're so busy they hardly have any time to do anything for patients. Like you're supposed to be able to talk to psychiatrists if you have any problems. But by the time you get around to seeing them your problem's solved itself one way or another. Like I knew my roommate was planning to commit suicide. She'd been talking about it, and I wanted to tell the head-shrinker so he could maybe stop her. Well, by the time I was up to see him the girl had already cut her throat with a razor.

"But I couldn't hold that against the psychiatrist. The only thing I hold against the whole staff is that they're so hopeless about you. They think once a junkie, always a junkie. And they don't mind letting you know it. Why, the day I was ready to go home, one of the nurses said, 'I expect I'll be seeing you soon, kid.' That hurt me, it really did."

Still, when Marilyn arrived home after four months, she was hopeful about herself. She had gained all her weight back. Her eyes were bright. She knew she looked well. Besides, she had taken part in some amateur dramatics while she was at Lexington, and she came home full of a great dream about studying to be an actress. She made an application to become a student at the Goodman Theatre but the directors refused to take her.

When her application to become a student was turned down, all the self-hatred she had been trying to stifle came to the fore. She thought, I'm good for nothing. I let my father and mother down. I slept with Denny. He was just a bum. No decent girl would have gone near him. And yet he was the one who threw me out. And now I can't be an actress. What can I be? What am I good for?

No one can know the agony with which a girl like Marilyn, always suspicious of her own inferiority, experiences the smallest of life's defeats. She is plunged into a hatred of herself from which she thinks there is but one escape.

On the day of the Goodman Theatre turndown, Marilyn felt she would commit suicide if she did not get her heroin. She felt a yen that was as overwhelming as any she had had before she went to Lexington. Her hands were shaking and her eyes were tearing. She was beginning to feel as physically sick as if she'd never been withdrawn from drugs. She could tell the nausea was about to hit her hard. And so she sought Denny out.

Denny was his old self. "Listen, Marilyn, you ain't no more to me than any other chick. I'll get you the stuff if you got the bread to pay me with."

Marilyn begged Denny: "Give me one shot on credit. For old time's sake."

"Like I told you before, I'm telling you again. Plenty of fellows I know would go for a girl like you." He chuckled. "I know how to get in touch with them for ten per cent of everything you make."

Marilyn said, "You can have the ten per cent, Denny. Can you get somebody for me right now, so I can have my shot?"

Today, three years after she first became hooked, Marilyn Green is a streetwalker. She is a sick woman at nineteen. She has served two jail sentences, one for possession of drugs, the other for prostitution. She has on one occasion returned to the hospital in Lexington. But, like the addicts she first met at Lexington, she has learned to circumvent the doctors there. Dope has deadened her feeling for everything else. Heroin has taken the place of remorse in her. Her mother and father are still "behind her" but the mother tells how, after Marilyn's last cure some six months ago, a social worker told her, "Mrs, Green, you ought to forget you have a daughter."

Chapter 3 You Beg When You're

Too Scared To Steal

Many young addicts come from the poor neighborhoods of big cities. As police officers have testified before Congressional committees, most druug arrests and violations of the drug laws occur in certain limited areas of cities, usually those areas of greatest social disorganization. These are the neighborhoods of poor and squalid housing, of overcrowding, of a shifting family life. They are the communities with the largest number of relief cases, the highest rates of juvenile delinquency, and of adolescent and adult crime. They are also the areas with the highest rates of mental disturbance and psychological abnormality. It is these disorganized slum neighborhoods, whether they exist in New York, Chicago, Los Angeles, Detroit or Washington, D.C., which develop a special cultural climate which is favorable to juvenile drug use as an escape from reality.

Many teen-age addicts are members of minority groups, Negro and Puerto Rican in the East and Mexican in the Southwest and Far West. To be a member of a minority group puts a person under specific social pressures. Negroes, Puerto Ricans and Mexicans have no social mobility. They nearly always must live within the confines of a caste system. We cannot ignore the effects of caste and discrimination on those who function at the bottom of the pile. They must of necessity be struggling with feelings of hatred, aggression, guilt, anxiety and—most of all—a strong retaliatory fear. They frequently learn to despise themselves and therefore to spurn their parents and the other authority figures in their lives. Naturally then, minority youngsters tend to grow up without either faith or trust in people.

Here is what many young addicts think about parents: "It would be better if they thought less about themselves and more about their kids. They don't want their kids to have any fun. They're always looking for things to nag their kids about." And about people generally: "You're a fool if you believe what most people try to tell you. Everybody is just out for himself. Nobody really cares about anybody else." And about the future: "The way things look for the future, most people would be better off if they were never born."

With such attitudes about life, it is understandable that young people will engage in a frantic search for newer, stranger, stronger intoxicants to give the illusion that they "have the world by the tail" and because heroin is the strongest and strangest intoxicant they have found to date, they cling to it with everything in them.

Angel Ricardo, seventeen years old, claims that he would kill himself if he were forced to do without his drug. He lives a different life from other boys of his age. School? Are you kidding? Work? What are you trying to put on Angel? Who'd hire a junkie? Begging and stealing, that's the play. You beg when you're too scared to steal and you steal when the begging time's bad.

Angel is like most addicts. He feels no union, no intimacy with anyone. When he was little, back in the old days in San Juan, Puerto Rico, he'd been full of love and tenderness for his father. At one time Angel felt pride and vanity because his father was big and strong. That had made up for the fact that he, himself, was small and thin. Angel had respected his father in the old days. Now, when he thinks of him at all, he thinks of him as a nonentity, "a nothing."

"What's my father got in his pocket anyhow?" he asks. "Money? No. Holes."

Somehow Angel's father had been different back in Puerto Rico, relaxed and high-spirited. He'd been used to laughing from way down inside. Or maybe it is merely Angel's vivid imagination. With addicts, you have no way of telling the difference between fact and imagination. But if you want to take Angel at his word, the father's downfall began on the plane between San Juan and New York. Bucket seats cost fifty dollars apiece in those days and the father had worked hard to ràise the three hundred dollars necessary for transporting the family—Angel, his two sisters, his mother and his grandmother.

"He was worrying all the way to New York," Angel tells, "wondering how we would live once we got there. But I didn't worry none then. I thought the old man was wonderful. I figured he could take care of us. He could do anything he wanted."

But, when the family landed at Idlewild Airport and it was freezing cold because it was winter, and when they stood around shivering in their light summer clothes, Angel began to doubt his father. Why didn't he get them the right clothes back home?

"Well," Angel's mother asked his father, "what do we do now?"

"I will ask how to get where we are going," the father said. "East 100th Street."

He went from person to person, trying to find someone who could understand his broken English. He held out the slip of paper on which was written the address of Angel's aunts and uncles in New York. But nobody understood what he was trying to say. Nobody made an effort to help him.

"I don't know, I don't know what to do," Angel's father told his mother.

"All right," the mother said, "you stay here with the children. "I'll find out myself how to get to the relatives' house." Her tone was derisive of her husband. She had never used such a voice in San Juan.

All the men looked as Angel's mother walked. She got the directions she sought without difficulty. Her success seemed to hurt Angel's father.

East 100th Street, where Angel's relatives lived, was a great disappointment. He had thought it would be a wide, beautiful, tree-lined street. He had dreamed about East 100th Street back home in San Juan. He was not prepared for what he saw, the ugly tenements and the garbage-lined sidewalks. His relatives in New York had lied when they wrote home.

"We are doing very well," they had said. "We are rich and successful. We have a beautiful home in New York."

Well, they could not be blamed for not being willing to reveal their poverty. But, now it was out in the open anyhow. They were embarrassed to be shown up. And because they were so uncomfortable, they behaved as though Angel and his family were strangers. They were not as Angel remembered them from San Juan. They spoke formally to his mother and father, and Angel's parents answered them the same way.

"How was your trip?"

"Fine."

"You must be tired."

"Yes."

"Angel, he's such a big boy now."

"Ah yes, the little ones grow big. And the big ones old."

After a couple of hours of such conversation, the relatives took Angel and his family to the apartment they had rented for them. It was two rooms in a cellar, located ten feet below street level. There was little ventilation. The rooms had once been coalbins. The walls were paper-thin.

"Well," Angel's father tried to speak cheerfully, "a little painting and polishing, a little fixing up here and there. . . ."

Angel's mother said, "People should not have to live in such a place."

The father said, "Don't worry. I'll get a job and we'll be out of here soon."

The mother laughed as though she did not believe him.

The old grandmother began to cry.

"Shut up," the father said.

Listening to his father and his grandmother, Angel felt sick. Life was strange when your father got so hard he wouldn't respect the older generation. If there is one value instilled in all Puerto Rican children from the time they are babies, it is respect for older people.

The grandmother kept telling Angel's father, "Shame, shame" and "your fault."

The father said, "You don't like it here, old woman? Go home again."

Angel had a terrible sensation. He wanted to warn his father to stop the bad talk before fate mowed him down. Father, remember this is Grandmother. But he couldn't bring the words out of his mouth. So he tried to concentrate on other things.

After a while, after months and years of living, a person grows accustomed to misery. It stops pounding on him. Angel would get up in the morning and do the things he had to. His father would too. Morning after morning he would look for a job. He never found one. The mother said he didn't really look. Angel's mother and father argued all the time and sometimes they fought with their fists. After a while, Angel got to where he did not pay any attention to their fights.

Angel's mother got herself a job in a garment shop downtown. She bought herself a couple of outfits, highheeled shoes and satin dresses. Angel didn't like his mother's new style. He thought she looked like a woman of the streets. It wasn't just her clothes either. It was the way she walked. And, after only a couple of months in New York, she grew tough and brutal around the house. She criticized Angel all the time.

Now Angel's grandmother cared for the house. She was old and sick and couldn't do much to keep the place clean. All day long she said her beads, gibbering with loneliness. Angel spent half his life avoiding her.

"Man," he says today, "she kept laying the same old story on me all the time. She wanted to go back to San Juan. It made me nervous to listen to her."

His grandmother was not the only one from whom Angel hid. He was always running away from the school authorities too. He felt stupid in the classroom. No matter how hard he studied it seemed that he couldn't remember what he'd learned. The teachers were always angry with him. After a while you couldn't drag Angel to school. The authorities threatened him with a correctional institution, but he yelled at them to bring it on because it couldn't be worse than the place they had him in already. Finally, for some reason he couldn't understand, the truant officers left him alone.

When he stopped going to school, Angel began living in a world of fantasy. He met a boy named Juan who introduced him to heroin and he soon found the narcotics dream more satisfying than real life. When he was high, he persuaded himself that his father had a good job and his mother looked respectable again. She didn't go to work. When Angel dreamed he did not see or hear anything he didn't want to. His old grandmother was happy. His living quarters were transformed. The family had plenty of rooms and enough good, clean beds to go around.

The best part of the dream concerned Angel himself. He didn't have to live his life out in the ghetto. He was welcome any place he wanted to go. He grew big and strong and he could talk as well as a teacher.

Actually, of course, Angel's mother grew more and more cocky with the power of her job. She always accused Angel and his father of ducking work. And Angel himself seemed riveted to the coalbin in which he lived. Once in a while he made a try at taking a walk outside his own neighborhood. And when he did, he heard the other boys yell, "Hey, Spick. Go back where you come from, you Spick bastard."

He wanted to stand up for his right to walk where he pleased. But he was afraid. So he always hurried back to his own territory. But he was not comfortable there, either. Many of the 100th street boys were as different from Angel as the downtowners were. Most of them belonged to gangs. They were brave and strong. They were the boys known around the street as "the bestest and the fastest." They were the "true hipsters." Because they were hip, many of them were "social junkers." They got together on week ends and "shot themselves full" of heroin. But they never became addicted. They could not afford to become addicted if they wanted to maintain their reputation as hipsters. On East 100th Street, to be hip means that you won't back off from anything, that you'll try everything for experience. But, by the same token, if you're a true hipster, nothing must get you down. So far as the drug is concerned, you must be able to take it or leave it alone. After all, you don't want to live your life out in a strait jacket, the way you have to if you're an addict.

Hipsters don't approve of addicts, and yet the Caballos, one of the most hip of the 100th street gangs, asked Angel to join them when he was sixteen years old. He was so proud he didn't know what to do. But his pride was soon knocked out of him. He found that even under the influence of the gang he couldn't be courageous. He was afraid to go on rumbles. He got nervous indigestion everytime he heard of one coming up. And he didn't like the gang shags. The young girls, lying around and waiting to be taken, disgusted him. He never got any thrill out of them.

In all the time Angel belonged to the Caballos, he didn't make a real friend. The other members never really liked or admired him. They only tolerated him. He never really felt himself one of them. He was always lonely.

So he began depending on the heroin more and more. After a while he gave up going to the Caballo clubroom. He got high whenever he could beg or steal the money. One time he was caught in the act of stealing a lady's pocketbook. He was arrested and his parents were sent for. His mother said he had always been unmanageable and his father backed her up with his silence. He was sent to the New York City Reformatory, where he kicked his habit and was taught a smattering of mechanics. But when he came out, he resumed his old habits—the stealing and the begging and the drugs.

"It is best to be junked up," he says. "That is when I feel good."

Chapter **4** **The Blues You Can't Lose**

Miraculously, there are boys and girls from underprivileged families and slum neighborhoods who are making a lot out of their lives. They manage to survive years of pain and misfortune. The Negroes who sing and play the blues are among such miracles of survival. Many of them are as disturbed as their peers. Their environment has created deep-rooted, major personality disorders in them. Like many of the boys with whom they grew up, they find it difficult to make friends, to feel close to people. And like the others they are sometimes overcome by a sense of futility, an expectation of failure. Yet they can go on clinging to their hope for a better world. It is because they love the blues. It is because they believe that through the blues they are interpreting their people to the world. They will tell you when you talk to them that the singing and the playing are their missions in life and that when a man has a mission, nothing can confound him or lay him low.

From the beginning there were people, including his own mother, who felt Jimmy Rogers was born to be either a thief or a pimp. On the other hand, there were some who believed he was born to make great music.

By the time he was nine years old, and looking younger because he was so underdeveloped, Jimmy was "in a groove" as far as the fly chicks, the prostitutes, and their sweet men were concerned. They said he had a doggy nose that could smell a good trick, and a fine vocabulary for signifying the score:

"You want to get your ashes hauled, Jack? You want to meet a saucy little chick?"

The prostitutes and their sweet men always loved Jimmy. It was a great pity his mother did not share their sentiments. Today Jimmy says. "She was a respectable one, spending most all of her time in church and with a big snout turned up at the fly chicks and their old men and at me, her own kid, because I loved to hang with them."

Whenever his mother was home she yelled at Jimmy —how come he ran away on Sunday morning just when it was time to go to church with her? And when, once in a while, she'd get him to go, why didn't he talk to the preacher like a little kid should? She'd ask why he looked "snooty and like he was gwine to take over the whole damn church—oh, God forgive me, I didn't mean to use them words, but the little devil with his heart full of evil starts in scuffling with me and this is what happens—I don't know what I'm saying, I don't know what I'm doing."

But Jimmy says he was not the one who started the scuffling. He says he never was and never would be.

"Just like my father never started the scuffling. He got fed up with it, though. One day, he chucked my old lady under her three chins and said:

" 'Bye-bye, baby. Plant you now and dig you later.' "

After his father left—Jimmy was eleven then—he had the "dismals." He says that even the fly chicks and their old men couldn't cheer him up. They'd strut by and summon him to follow. But he wouldn't go. He'd sit on the stoop and watch them out of sad eyes.

"Daddy-o, Daddy-o, come home to me now."

Damn, damn, damn his old man. He hadn't said goodbye to Jimmy, but only to the old lady. And all the time Jimmy had thought he'd loved him best of all.

"Bye-bye, baby. Plant you now and dig you later."

When, Pa, when? Dig *me*, huh? She don't want you to

dig her. She don't want you to like her or know what she's really like inside.

Jimmy had always known his mother didn't want to be dug, not by his pa or any other mortal man. Oh, by some mortal man, maybe; that preacher she was always talking about. Pa used to tell it to the old lady during the days, every single day, when he was troubled with the shorts, had not red cent one and she wouldn't give him any money but saved it all for the church collection box.

"Hey, Minnie Mae, how come the preacher's Mr. Kingpin now? Ain't *my* loving good enough?"

"Loving? Loving? I done outgrown you, boy."

"Since when you done outgrown me, Minnie Mae?"

"Since the day I given my heart to God."

"Aw, Minnie Mae, come on, baby. I ain't asking so much. Give me a deuce, will you, huh?"

"Get out of here, lazybones. Get yourself a job like other men do."

"Honey, listen to me, sweet, it ain't no good. My feet's too long out of work."

"Well, my feet's sick and sore from working and waiting on you and that kid of yourn."

"You ain't talking like a ma, Minnie Mae. It's all right when you start in laying the mess on me. But what the hell you laying it on the boy? He ain't only mine. He's yourn too."

"So what if he's mine too? That don't give me no cause for feasting. He's grown like you and not like me. I ought to whup his nappy head."

Jimmy left the house when his father and mother fought over him. He'd go looking for the fine chippies, the fly chicks and their sweet men. Actually he wasn't looking for them either; he was looking for something else, for someone to help bring out the music that beat in his brain.

In the days when Jimmy was growing up, there was a house on 137th Street and Lenox Avenue. It wasn't like any other house and it wasn't like the homes of the plain chicks who used to work on their own. It had three sharptogged prostitutes in it. And then there was Birdie Blair. Jimmy says she was just an old mama-stringbean. But she could play the piano and she could give out with a song to make your heart flutter and tremble. Sometimes she sang some of the old Bessie Smith numbers and when she did, there was a little of the great Bessie someplace inside her.

> "See that long, lonesome road, Lawd, you know it's gotta end."

Sometimes Birdie composed songs to make your burden light. Once in a while she'd compose one for Jimmy.

> "You got a overdose of troubles, Jimmy Boy,
> And so I got some talk for you
> Don't let nothing get you worried, don't let nothing get you down.
> Make it, boy. Sing. Sing oo-oo-wee."

As she sang to Jimmy, the healing love poured out of Birdie. She was able to soothe all the boy's troubles away. Troubles? Here, with Birdie Blair, Jimmy couldn't remember any troubles. Ma and Pa didn't matter. Neither did his dreams and nightmares.

Only last night, Jimmy had wakened screaming. A giant with a head of fire had stood beside his bed. He'd called for his mother, but she was off at one of her religious meetings. He'd called for his father, but he was off for good and all.

> "Oh Papa, Papa, where are you at tonight,
> Your sonny's got the deep-down, deep-down blues."

The next morning he'd sung his song to Birdie.

"Kid," she said, "what I mean, you're *vibrating*, boy." She sat down at the piano and banged out an accompaniment for the tune he had devised.

Jimmy's head buzzed as he listened. His body shook all over. This was *it*. This was *the life*.

Soon, the lonely nights stopped worrying him. Whenever he'd get keyed up, he'd start composing his blues in the night. The mad music churned around in his mind, exciting him. It was only after he had sung his songs to Birdie that the excitement died down and the relaxed feeling took its place.

Birdie was wonderful. She taught Jimmy to play the piano. She said the spirit of the music was in him. The spirit? That was the relief that made Jimmy able, all of a sudden, to talk to the world. Even to his mother. The hardness left her when she heard him sing. Then she would act soft and soulful, like a woman and not a man, like his mother and not his enemy.

But his mother didn't matter any more. Birdie Blair had taken her place in Jimmy's life. She spent all her free time playing and singing for him. And she talked with him a lot. She jived with everyone else around her. But she always told Jimmy the truth about the music having to be his mother, father, friend and lover. Hell, some cats need chicks for getting gone with. Some need whiskey. Some need junk. But if you've got the music you can get gone without the chicks, or the whiskey or the junk. Don't matter how drug out you are, child, you begin singing about what's in your heart and all of a sudden you're feeling good all over, body and soul.

She told Jimmy that the music was the poetry of his people. It's the laughing underneath the crying that makes the music great. Godalmighty, white folks can't know about the laughing underneath the crying. They think the blues is all crying, no laughing. Don't forget the laughing underneath the crying. When you sing the blues, you gotta bubble inside. Oh yes, one thing more, when you're looking around for folk you're going to like, see to it that those people live in your world. They got to know what the blues are all about. If they don't understand the blues, they don't understand you.

After many years of Birdie Blair's tutoring, Jimmy managed to connect with the best blues bunch in all of Harlem, New York. Big Chinchy Johnson was the leader. Chinchy was a good leader and a fine businessman. He took Jimmy under his wing.

Chinchy always dressed well. One day he took Jimmy to his tailor. After that, Jimmy dressed well too. He got to be a fashion plate. All the women hung around him.

Still and all, he never wanted a permanent girl. The

music always came first. He figured that only lone men could moan the woeful blues. He often thought that if he hadn't been so sad and alone when he was younger, he'd never have begun the singing.

Chinchy Johnson was the only one in the world except Birdie Blair to whom Jimmy told his story. Maybe that was why Chinchy induced Jimmy to take his first puff of marijuana.

"The weed'll help you come on, kid. It'll help the weeps and it'll help the laughs."

Chinchy was right. Jimmy felt himself a fine singer when he had the "salt and pepper" in him.

"Like, dig," he explains, "my songs came zooming out of me down-home solid. I was sure of myself. I looked out and saw those cats and chickens eating me up. I was *singing*. Nothing would ever mess me up no more. Well, like I got a headache later on. But it didn't matter none.

"After that first night, I smoked tea all the time. I blew my lump. I got sent. All the same it wasn't like I was on the wicked stuff. It ain't like you're smoking hop or inhaling snow when you're sipping tea. Hell, it ain't like you're getting all filled up with horse. You sip tea, you don't get a habit. Anybody knows that. Nothing's wrong with sipping tea—except one thing. You can go to jail for it."

One Saturday night, two white men came up onto the platform from which Jimmy was singing and showed their copper badges. They searched him for reefers and took him down to the station house.

Jimmy was high on marijuana when he first left with the officers. But after a while the effect of his reefers wore off. His stomach churned and all he could think of was, if they keep me in jail with no chance to get at the music I'll go off my rocker.

"Like, dig," he says, "the law locked me up in a ratty cell and I kept pacing up and down all night long—one two, one two. I don't know, I was so low down. Well, I come up for trial in Special Sessions Court and a couple coppers came and tried with all the tricks in their pates to get me to lay the blame on the other cats. Say, they told me, I wanted out, didn't I? Well then, who was using? Who was selling? I told them, 'look, you puny little police-

men, you can try stretching my noodle from here to king-
dom come but you ain't gwine get word one out'n my mouth.
Dig,' I says. 'I ain't no handkerchief-head square.' Well, one
of them Rover Boys, he says. 'I got news for you, kid. You
better start laying that handkerchief on your head this minute or you might end up with a long bit.' I told them I
ain't gwine lay. You should've seen them blowtops laughing.
'Listen, black boy, you know how we knew you had all
that tea?' It seems one of my own cats was the one turned
rat on me. I said, 'Don't try to put that mess down.' One
of the Rover Boys, he said, 'Boy, you act like you was born
yesterday or something. You think your pals is deadbeat
as you are? You think your pals'd take the rap for you just
like you're going to be taking it for them? Are you really
all that dumb or are you just putting on?' I acted like I
didn't believe a word. But all the time I was bugged up.
Which razor-legged obscenity went and turned me in?

"Well, at my trial them pounders snapped their caps and
skullbusted the judges. What do you think—they said I
wasn't just a viper but also scumpteen of a pusher. A pusher,
huh? If that was the case, how come I had the twos and
fews? Hell, where was all my sawbucks, where was all my
green at? I guess those judges weren't wallering in all they
told him because they only give me sixty days. Only sixty.
For what? For trillying and drinking the tea, that's all.
Hell, like here's a solid fact, no crack—I have yet to hear
from anybody that tea's bad for a person. None of them
croakers scuffling around was able to put tea down along
with the wicked stuff would give you a habit. How come
I was getting sent up, then?

"They sent me up to Rikers. What's the use talking about
Rikers? It's a *jail*, that's all. Just like any other jail. I kept
a lot of rumpus and still I had some bad times. A couple
times looked like the bars had got wound around and was
like to choke the breath out of me. That was when I got
word that Chinchy was killed in an automobile accident. I
was like to blow my top. A bug doctor got me then and
give me the business. But, I soon got on my rocker and
started in flying right again. This bug doctor I'm talking
about, some of the hopheads used to go and see him and
maybe I'd've kept on going to him. But we had a mug of

a screw was always lowrating anybody went to see the bug doctor.

" 'Hey, Simpy, the bug doctor's calling for you. How come the bug doctor wants *you*, kid? You freakish?' I might have kept seeing that bug doctor if I hadn't've fell into the mouth of that screw. I knew I was complexy and the bug doctor was opening things up. Man, it's crazy. The city pays all that bread out to the doctor and then the screw makes you feel like a big moron if you go to him. But who's talking about that now? Who's talking about the inside? It's what happened on the outside that give me the blues you can't lose. It's what happened after I walked and all."

As soon as he got of jail, Jimmy went looking around for another singing job. He thought he wouldn't have much trouble finding one. Everyone knew he was the greatest. Plenty of leaders had tried to steal him away from Chinchy in the good old days. But now they all gave him the same story:

"Man, I'm sorry. I can't use you."

"How come?"

"You can't work without'n you got your police card."

That's how it is with entertainers. Once you get collared, the police take away your player's police identification card. You must have a police card if you're going to work in a cabaret or any other spot where liquor is sold. So Jimmy went down to the police and tried to get his card back.

"Well," he tells, "I was soon feeling gully-low. The gimpies told me no, I couldn't have my license."

"But why," he asked over and over again, "why the hell you sending me on this rugged road for?"

All his talking did him no good.

When Jimmy arrived home after his bout with the police, he went to see the pals he'd played with in Chinchy's band.

"They went hincty on me too. Those cats jumped stink on their own boy. They was better than brothers to me in the old days and now they jumped stink. They clammed tight. Talk about a bringdown."

Still, Jimmy knew he had no right to become angry. The fact was, his men would have liked to have helped him out but they were afraid that if they did a stool pigeon might tell an officer.

"Hey, So-and-So's hanging with Jimmy now." And, next thing you know, the officer would be watching Jimmy's friend.

"So, when a fellow loses his police card," Jimmy says, "his friends have to get smart and run away from him."

Now Jimmy could neither sing the blues nor listen to the music he loved. Besides, he was broke. Perhaps it was only natural that he should start pushing the marijuana and taking the heroin. At first he played around with the heroin, thinking he was too smart to get hooked. He didn't mainline except on Saturdays and Sundays. On weekdays, he smoked marijuana.

And then, one Friday night, his mouth felt dry, his eyes filled up with tears and he began feeling like he had to heave. He was hip. He knew the yen for what it was. "All right, so I'm hooked. All right, so I am. Without the music, what the hell do I have to hold out for? What's the difference what I do with my life?"

Chapter 5   Man Among Men

There are some addicts who could never be recognized as such. They are not pale-faced or emaciated. The pupils of their eyes are not pin-pointed. They are not lethargic or sleepy or stuporous. Many of them who take drugs regularly, but are able to refrain from excessive dosage, maintain normal lives over the years. There are government officials, business leaders and professional men among them. So long as they have the drug they need they function well at work and in society.

Dr. Allen Mall is an unrecognizable addict. He is six feet tall, solid and husky. He works hard—ten, eleven, twelve hours a day.

"I take morphine," he says in his clipped speech. "Six grains every day. I've been on the habit for fourteen years. As you can see, I am in good health. I would venture to say that my motor control and my critical judgment are as good as anybody's. I am not fearful of treating patients. Why should I be? So long as I have my dosage of the drug, I am a normal man and a good, careful doctor. Of course I hesitate to think what I would be if I were denied the morphine. Certainly I would be too weak to work. Not because of any physical dependence, mind you, but rather because I become depressed when I don't have morphine.

I am terrified of the depression. I go to pieces when I think of it."

There is something strange about Allen Mall, M.D., that must strike one at sight. There is a brooding isolation about him. He looks like a man who has fought and lost life's battle.

"Some people," he says, "are born frightened."

Little Allen Mall was always full of fear. He was shaky about meeting people and he was scared of the dark. Sometimes he'd waken at night crying and his bare, cold feet would carry him straight into his mother's room. To him, when he was growing up, the room had always been his mother's, never his father's.

"Mommy."

"What, baby?"

"I'm scared."

"Ssh, you'll wake your father."

His father. Every time he looked at the big, heavy man-form under the bulging bedclothes, he got a sick feeling.

"Mommy, come to my room."

"No."

Young as he was, he knew that she wanted to come. He knew that all he had to do was weep a little and then she'd come wherever he wanted her to. Not that his tears were faked. A boy who's always quivering inside doesn't have to fake tears. They come naturally.

"I'm scared, Mommy."

"What of?"

"Everything." He kneeled down by her side of the bed and started kissing the cover. She could never resist that act.

"All right, baby, come on."

Even in the dark, Allen could make out his mother's figure in the clinging nightgown. This was it. She was coming. Another minute, another two minutes and she'd be in his room with him. He'd lean against her. And then she'd take him in her arms and press her mouth against his and stroke his neck gently, tenderly. What in the world could compare to the wonderful luxury of being stroked to sleep by her work-calloused hands? He loved the feel of their hardness.

But sometimes his father came in unexpectedly and then

his mother apologized for being in Allen's room. Allen felt jealous and rejected when his father came.

His father was a big brute of a man who made his living by the sweat of his brow. It annoyed him that Allen didn't seem to take after him. He used to say, "I don't want no son of mine growing up to be a *sissy*."

Allen's mother defended him from the dreadful word.

"Oh, God, I swear you must be going crazy. A sissy? Allen? Believe me, you don't know your own boy."

"Maybe you're the one don't know him."

"Oh no, that's a good one, it really is. Let me ask you something; you ever watch that 'sissy' in the park or in the playground? You ever see him shinnying up trees? You ever look at him swinging?"

Allen's mother was right and his father wrong, more or less. Allen was brave at the playground. He was a whiz at shinnying up trees. He tried all kinds of tricks on the swings.

"Look, Mommy, I'm swinging."

"Baby, I see you. I see you, sweetie."

Her smile made up for the fear he felt as he swung. I'll fall, Ma, I'm falling. Catch me, Ma, I'll die. Pa would like me to.

Allen did everything for his mother. He felt he had to. He won all the honors in elementary and high school and walked off with a college scholarship. His mother really rode the high horse then.

Allen did not like college. He hated being away from his mother. Nobody knew it, of course. He still stole the honors and awards. But they all led up to one thing—coming home to mother on his vacation and seeing the pride in her eyes when he discussed his college activities with her. Allen loved every minute he spent with her. He even did girls' tasks just to be in her presence. He enjoyed setting the table, for instance. And, when nighttime came, he might still walk into her room.

"Ma?"

"What's wrong, son?"

"I—I have a headache."

"Go to bed, dear. I'll bring you some aspirin."

Back in his room, he thought of how wonderful his

mother was. While he waited for her, he switched the light out, figuring, I'd rather she'd be with me in the dark.

She turned the light back on when she came. Damn her for that. She sat on the side of his bed. He wanted her to put her hand on his head, to touch him.

"I never had such an awful headache."

"Is it all over your head, or only on one side?"

What was she asking questions for? Why didn't she just put her hand where he wanted it? "One side."

"Which one?"

"The right." He got out of bed and leaned against her. She pressed her mouth against his hair. It was good to feel it there. And then, suddenly, something occurred in him. He jerked his neck from under her gently stroking hand and a spasm of anger twisted his handsome face.

"You're as bad as some of the dames I know. Always trying to kiss me."

The girls were always trying to kiss him too. And they protested loudly when he refused their passes. He knew they gossiped about him.

Allen was twenty-one years old when he entered medical school. He also met Paula Leonard that year. She was a fat, flabby woman of forty. Her oldest son was Allen's own age. Allen was drawn to Paula from the day he met her. At first he refused to recognize his passion. He tried to destroy it. He examined the woman for imperfections. She was old enough to be his mother. She was clumsy. She was stumpy. Her clothes were so terrible people giggled at her in the street.

And still, although he put his mind to stifling the love he felt, nothing made any difference. He couldn't overcome it.

Paula, for her part, was not drawn to Allen. She thought he was strange. She always complained about the places he took her to.

"The food stinks. The chef's lousy."

"I'm sorry, darling."

"Why don't you find out what a place is like before you take me there?"

"I will from now on."

"That's what you always say."

"I'm sorry, darling."

"Yeah, you're always sorry, too."

Once he asked her, "Do we have to quarrel every time we're together?"

"If you don't like me, Allen, why don't you go out with one of your young ingenues who'll look up to you, no matter what you do?"

"I don't want any young ingenues. I want you, Paula. Do you want me, too?"

"I don't mind going out with you."

He could never determine whether her indifference was real or simulated. It infuriated him.

"Listen, Paula, don't you care about me one way or the other?"

"Well, no, Allen, I don't."

No matter what insult she threw at him, it still did not affect his love. For several years he groveled before her.

Once in a while she would let him make love to her. But there was no sensuality in the woman. She would lie in bed looking bored. At those times he would feel the burden of his shaky masculinity. And yet he could not leave her.

When he graduated from medical school and finished his internship, he asked her to divorce her husband and marry him. She laughed at him.

"Marry you? I'm not out of my mind yet."

"But why, Paula? I love you so much."

"Listen, I got to be married to a *man*."

"I'll be a doctor. Doctors make money. I'll be able to give you everything you ever wanted."

"I already told you, you can't give me the thing I want more than money. You can't be a man."

"Paula, what are you talking about?"

"Go home, little boy. Don't bother me."

A couple of weeks after Paula sent him away, Allen met Anita Howard. She was a kindly, thoughtful, generous girl. And very pretty. Besides, she saw Allen with a halo around his head.

One time, after they had known each other several months, she said, "Allen, I want to ask you a question. Maybe it'll embarrass you. In a way, I'm humiliated to be asking it.

But I will, anyhow. Do you love me at all, Allen? Because I love you so awfully."

It was hard for Allen to realize once and for all that he couldn't love that clean, slender, pretty girl but still longed for the touch of a slut he couldn't have. It forced him to face the problem that had been beating on him since he was a boy. He saw himself as a "lonesome freak." In all his life, he had been able to make contact with only two people, not counting his mother: Paula and Anita. But he couldn't stick to either of them. Sometimes he felt as though he were wearing a sign reading "Quarantine." Other people could live together. They sustained one another through their hard times. Why did he have to go through life by himself?

Allen's mother died two years after Paula kicked him out. He went into a deep depression and began taking morphine after he came out of it.

"I can honestly say the drug helped me to survive," he says. "Yes, it's a crutch. And I'm a cripple. Sick. Soul-sick. I would be the first to admit there's something rotten in me. But with my daily dose of morphine I'm a man among men. I'm a human being. I can hold on to my dignity. I'm a good doctor, not in spite of the rotten core, but rather because of it. As I have no life of my own, I have a greater dedication than most other doctors. You see, I must live for my work since I have nothing else. And, another thing. I don't want to sound immodest, but the issue's important enough so I must be truthful: Without morphine, I would be a burden on society. With morphine, I am making a contribution of which I am proud. I often wonder how many other addicts could be leading constructive lives if they were not deprived of their succor. That *is* something to ponder."

Chapter 6 Larceny, Shoplifting Sneak Thievery

Numerous eminent doctors have reported about addicts of the type of Dr. Mall. Their studies prove that the use of drugs does not substantially impair the efficiency of addicts, but rather that it is the lack of the drug and the constant preoccupation with obtaining it that turns addicts into what we are accustomed to think of as "the typical addict personality."

Dr. Lawrence Kolb, foremost medical authority on drug addiction, has said that many prominent people who lead socially useful lives and are able to function effectively in their business or professions are long-term addicts. Significantly, one would not be able to recognize most of them as users.

Drs. Abraham Wikler and Charles Rasor, writing in the *American Journal of Medicine*, add to Dr. Kolb's statement. They say that many users believe that drugs *improve* their ability to do useful work and that under the influence of opiates they "keep out of trouble." While it is certainly difficult to verify such statements of users, the doctors say that observations made under experimental conditions are in substantial agreement with them.

"As long as adequate amounts of opiates are administered," Drs. Wikler and Rasor conclude, "aggressive antisocial behavior is practically never observed, personal hygiene is maintained, assigned responsibilities are discharged satisfactorily."

Of course, this is not to say that opiate addiction is either moral or socially desirable or that we ought not to discourage it. But addiction is only a symptom of a person's general illness. The drug addict does not fall sick because he takes drugs. Rather he takes them because he *is* sick. And an hysterical press and public which feels that attention should be directed to the drug itself rather than to the total personality of the user is merely obscuring the fundamental issue. An isolated attack on drug use is bound to fail.

Who is the typical addict? Actually, there is no typical addict. There is a constant interplay of individual factors at work in determining who will succumb to addiction. We know, for example, that in Harlem and similar slum areas of large cities there is a good deal of casual usages of drugs, that some street-gang boys like the 100th Street Caballos take heroin only two or three times a week, some even less often. We know that they take it as part of a leisure-time pattern, part of a social activity. Nobody knows why they, who have been exposed to the same kinds of basic problems as the addicted boys like Angel Ricardo, the same early upbringing, the same parental conflicts, the same social conflicts, can experiment with narcotics and never become addicts. Psychiatrists do not have the answer. They say that the only clear conclusion they have come to about addicts is that they take drugs to help them overcome certain personality deficiencies which make it difficult or impossible for them to cope with the real world in which they live. Psychiatrists say addicts must have their drugs so that they may avoid the anxieties and tensions that arise from family conflicts, sex conflicts or social difficulties, and, if they are adolescents, their need to grow up and take their place in a normal world. The psychiatrists' thesis may be proved by examination of those gangs which have experimented with drugs for "kicks."

According to a study conducted in 1956 by New York University entitled "Heroin Use and the Street Gang" most youngsters as they grow older lose their interests in delinquent activities, gang fights and drugs for kicks. Instead, they become concerned about their futures, thinking in terms of jobs, marriage and fatherhood.

"But for those gang members who are too disturbed emotionally to face the future as adults," the report reads, "the passing of adolescent hell-raising leaves emptiness, boredom, apathy and restless anxiety. In a gang where there are many such disturbed members, experimentation with drugs for 'kicks' will soon lead to frequent and, later, habitual use; cliques of users will grow quickly. Enmeshed in the patterns of activities revolving around the purchase, sale and use of drugs and the delinquent efforts to get money to meet the exorbitant cost of heroin, the young users can comfortably forget about girls, careers, status and recognition in the society at large. Their sexual drive is diminished, they maintain a sense of belonging in the limited world of the addict, they remain children forever. They may give up all sense of personal responsibility for their lives and conveniently subject the blame for their shiftless existence on 'the habit.' "

Fundamentally, many drug users are emotionally immature and have never made a proper adaptation to the problems of living as adults. At the same time, their personalities run the gamut of the standard psychiatric nomenclature from the simple anxiety states to the major psychoses. Doubtless, if they did not take drugs they would find other means of expressing their conflicts. This statement of a young but long-term addict is not atypical:

"I was always getting into trouble before I got on drugs —never could seem to get comfortable; I had to go somewhere and do something all the time. I was always in trouble with the law. Some fellows told me about drugs and how good they made you feel, and I tried them. From then on, I was content, as long as I had my drugs—I didn't care to do anything but to sit around, talk to my friends occasionally, listen to the radio, and only be concerned with the problems of getting money for drugs. This I usually did by picking pockets or other such petty stuff."

Some experts blame addiction on social conditions. Alfred Cohen, Director of the Warwick Training School for Boys, said at a conference on drug addiction among adolescents, held at the New York Academy of Medicine:

"Ten years from now I doubt that we shall have the narcotics problem but we shall have another problem. I can't begin to guess what it will be, but we shall always have problems among adolescents in the city of New York, where we have hideous social conditions and slum areas like Harlem and East Harlem."

It was in Harlem that detectives of the New York City Narcotic Squad found an eight-year-old boy who said he had been smoking marijuana for a year.

"We don't know whether he had been smoking it or not," said Inspector Peter Terranova, head of the Squad until recently, "but he certainly gave us a good story about the effects of the use of marijuana. We believe either someone had given him a detailed story or he *had* been smoking. He told us from whom he was purchasing. There were three groups. There were the seniors, the juniors and the midgets and he was a midget. The midgets would purchase marijuana from the juniors. Where the juniors obtained it, we could not ascertain. They would not permit him to go with the juniors. The juniors purchased marijuana and heroin from the seniors. We picked up the boy from whom the eighty-year-old was supposed to have gotten the marijuana; he was sixteen. Of course he said he did not know anything about it, and so we stepped with him into a hallway, stripped up the sleeves of his jacket and found hypodermic needle marks on his arms— sixteen years old. Further questioning disclosed his source of supply as a nineteen-year-old youth. . . ."

The nineteen-year-old peddler pointed out a Harlem hallway which he said twelve teen-agers used as a shooting gallery. Agents searched the hallway and came up with an eye dropper, a needle and a cap of heroin. Of course they could not prove ownership. They also picked up the twelve boys.

"The best we could do was take them in, take their names and addresses and send for their parents. I was surprised at how little the parents seemed to know or care about their children's habits. It was as though someone else, not they themselves, should have been concerned."

Inspector Terranova's view of the general indifference on the part of parents of adolescent narcotics users is substantially the same as that of Judge Peter Horn, who has met many addicts' families in his twenty years of service in the New York City Magistrates' Courts:

"There are many parents in this town who realize their youngsters are taking drugs, and either they are inadequate to cope with the problem or they are ashamed and take no steps. When we bring evidence to the parents, their indifference is amazing. I think that is another indication of how much there is that we don't know."

What does an addict get out of his addiction? Doctors have found that the use of opiates reduces pain and erotic urges of all sorts. In addition, intravenous injection gives a transient "thrill." After there effects have developed, a sense of gratification or satisfaction is achieved and addicts feel more at ease and free to do what they "want to do." Some may want to doze peacefully and enjoy daydreams of wealth, power or social prestige. Others may want to socialize. One important effect most addicts describe is the new comfort they feel in the presence of members of the opposite sex.

Opium is the source from which heroin and morphine, the chief drugs used by addicts, are derived. It is a dark, gummy substance secured from the dried juice of the unripe seed pod of the opium poppy. All opium derivatives are depressants, drugs which induce mental and physical relaxation. Morphine and heroin are sold in powder form on the illegal market, in strengths that depend on how much individual sellers wish to make on their supplies, the strength of which they themselves do not know. They dilute them and package them in capsules, paper packets, pills or cubes. Both heroin and morphine are highly addicting. They can be sniffed or dissolved in fluid for injection under the skin or into a vein.

The only two drugs used by addicts today that do not result in a physical dependence are marijuana and cocaine. Marijuana is made from the flowers and leaves of a plant which may be grown in nearly any climate. It is sometimes cultivated surreptitiously in some of the empty lots of our own big cities. It produces an effect similar to an alcoholic binge, causing the user to act silly but feel clever. Jazz musicians like Jimmy Rogers have been attracted to it in the erroneous belief that it improves their performances. Marijuana users have no withdrawal symptoms when their high wears off. They gradually return to normal, much as alcoholics do. Marijuana, unlike the opium derivatives, releases the mental controls that keep aggressiveness in check. Thus that drug can produce antisocial behavior while the user is under its influence, and can and often does lead a person to attempts at finding new thrills with heroin.

Cocaine, obtained from coca leaves, is a true stimulant and a pain reliever. It is taken either by sniffing or injection. It produces a feeling of intense pleasure, fatigue disappears, and the user feels strong and superior. Some addicts mix it with heroin.

There is comparatively little use of cocaine and marijuana among either adolescents or adults. There is some marijuana smoking, of course, and there are also a minor number of users who sniff odd mixtures of cocaine and morphine. But by and large the bulk of addicts are heroin users who have graduated from "skin-popping," shooting the heroin into any part of the body, to "mainlining," shooting it directly into a vein.

Mainliners heat the heroin in a teaspoon over a small flame, draw it up into a dropper and inject it into the vein by means of a hypodermic needle which has been attached to the dropper. These instruments are known as "the works." Some addicts who cannot obtain hypodermic needles use safety pins for puncturing their veins. Usually ulcers form around the parts of the body where there have been many injections. Sometimes, due to an unsanitary set of works, the ulcers become infected. Addicts have been known to die from such infections.

People, particularly parents and schoolteachers, often ask how it is possible to spot adolescent addicts. That is a difficult question. Many professionals, such as court probation officers, oriented as they are to conduct intelligent inquiries and look for the right signs, admit that some addicts, even full-fledged ones, get past them.

Dorris Clarke, chief probation officer of the New York City Magistrates' Courts, stated at the conference on drug addiction at the New York Academy of Medicine that "our addicts are now quite accustomed to the fact that we examine their arms and legs, so are shooting themselves in the abdomen, buttocks, and behind the knees. We have had to extend our instructions for physical examination. The thing that has caused me considerable concern in the past month is that four cases have gone across my desk for discharge from probation because the defendant died from an overdose of heroin. No matter how carefully we have examined, and how carefully we have pursued them under supervision, there is nothing in our records to indicate they were even using drugs; and I am more than ever convinced that a large proportion of this problem is that we don't know about it, that there seems to be a certain amount of resilience about adolescents. Certainly all drug users are pathological liars. The hardest thing in the world is to get the truth from them, but I currently have four cases in which there was no indication of any use of drugs, no indication of association with users of drugs, and they have been found dead in furnished rooms and diagnosed by the City toxicologist as having died from an overdose of heroin. That is causing us considerable concern."

And yet, parents and teachers, spending hours with their children, and with a particular sensitivity to them, can often succeed where the professionals fail. That is not to say that they will be unwaveringly correct in picking out signs of addiction, especially before it has become well established. It is unfortunate that most users cannot be discovered in the early stages, because it is then that they may possibly be diverted from becoming true addicts.

A user who has recently begun to take heroin (he's not yet an addict) or one who may have been "joy-popping," not mainlining, for a longer period, loses the drug's effect in a few hours and then appears to be more or less himself. The heroin causes no deviation from his normal routine, except that he may seem somewhat subdued and easy-going and somewhat talkative in a quiet, self-contented way. He generally seems pleased with himself and his surroundings. His eyes may be the most obvious sign of his use. The pupils are generally pin-pointed and will not enlarge in dim light.

If a user is encountered when "high," however, he will be sleepy, slow-moving, lethargic, possibly stuporous, and dreamy. He will be "goofing," nodding off in short periods of sleep, while fantasying on a grandiose scale. If he does not resort only to snorting or sniffing, he will show in addition needle marks on his body. Of course, the finding of the "works" makes his condition obvious. So does examination of his urine, where evidence of the drug may show up to ten days after its last use.

Once a person becomes a true addict, his family will no

longer have to wonder about him. They will be bound to notice the marked change in his behavior and personality. He will most likely lose weight, not from any physical deterioration, but because he loses appetite and fails to consume a proper amount of food. His behavior will be marked chiefly by what has come to be known as "the addict's routine." He will be driven by a constant, persistent pressure to get the drug. His daily life will become geared to getting money for the drug and nothing else. Every other obligation, interest, activity which formerly was part of family life, school routine or work activity will lose meaning for him and become replaced by a frantic effort to beg, steal or borrow each day enough money to make a buy. He will lose his interest in his "square" friends, and in his appearance. He will become sullen and withdrawn and will spend long hours alone. He will be intolerant of other peoples' wishes or of any kind of restraint on his activities. He will lie, deceive, and connive to get his "junk."

Simultaneously with the development of these marked personality changes, he will have become physically dependent on the drug, and the so-called abstinence or withdrawal syndrome will develop if he is forced to stop using drugs. The fear of the abstinence syndrome or the withdrawal illness is the pressure which can drive the addict out of his mind. He will do anything to avoid the running nose, the tearing eyes, the sweats, the chills, the muscular and abdominal cramps, the involuntary twitches and shakes and kicks, the back pain, the vomiting.

The fact should have been faced a long time ago that once a user has actually recognized himself as an addict subject to withdrawal pain, he will let nothing stand in the way of maintaining a constant supply of his drug. He will not be stopped in his compulsion by any threat, including that of prison.

Our thinking about drug addiction is primitively oversimplified. Our law-enforcement authorities consider it a vice and maintain that it can be overcome if a person makes a sufficient effort. Despite the testimony of eminent doctors, psychiatrists and social workers as to its inefficacy, they use the threat of jail with the addict. And, as was illustrated in the case of Marilyn Green, they do not allow doctors to give him treatment. No wonder an addict must seek his succor from the underworld instead of from legitimate society. And, of course, the price that the underworld exacts from him is so high that he is practically mandated to become a criminal.

How, except through criminal activity, can a person with a twenty-, thirty-, forty-, fifty-dollar-a-day habit and no particular wealth or talent raise the money he needs? By larceny, shoplifting, sneak thievery, dope pushing and prostitution. These are the crimes to which drug addicts inevitably turn. We ought to be thankful that the vast majority of them do not have the courage, the stamina or the disposition to commit murder, armed robbery and other crimes of violence. Otherwise, thanks to our narcotics laws, addicts would not merely resort to their traditional parasitic and predatory crimes, they would also threaten the general security and well-being of society by committing more serious crimes.

BOOK II

Anatomy
of
a Mob

Chapter **1** Mafia

Who are the familiar yet enigmatic moguls of the underworld whom narcotics addicts keep in business? In order to understand narcotics mobsters, who must first try to probe the working of Mafia, the death-giving organization which spawned the great majority of them, and which takes in well over three billion dollars a year from illegal enterprises. Its tactics, with its own membership as well as outsiders, are vastly puzzling. Mafia walks on silent feet. Its operations are extremely devious.

On May 2, 1957, one of the Mafia masterminds, the notorious racketeer Frank Costello, was shot at by an unknown assassin. As it happened, the bullet merely creased his scalp and ricocheted off the wall. Still, the question remains unanswered as to who tried to kill Costello. The police were plagued with cock-and-bull stories and one resulting prosecution of a Mafia hoodlum ended in an acquittal. The most credible story was that of the rift between Costello and Big Al Anastasia, head of the Mafia police force and one-time lord high executioner of Murder, Inc. Those in the know were aware that Big Al had been trying for years to take over some of the gambling preserves that the Mafia had granted Costello and that the big Mafiosi, composing the Grand Council of the organization, did not like his activities. Big Al was also trying to muscle in on the Cuban territory of Meyer Lansky and his silent gambling partner, the then dictator Fulgencio Batista.

"I do not want Anastasia in Cuba," Batista is reputed to have told the American underworld.

And Anastasia is said to have answered, "I will go to Cuba no matter what Batista says. Tell him that."

Anastasia never got to go. On October 25, 1957, he was shot dead in the barbershop of the Hotel Park Sheraton in New York City. Who murdered Anastasia? Police questioning brought no information. However, they are certain the assassin is a Mafioso.

On November 14, 1957, some time after the two gangland shootings, sixty-five Mafia tycoons were surprised in a secret meeting at the Apalachin, New York, home of gangman Joseph Barbara. What were they doing there? Just fulfilling social amenities. Their friend Barbara had fallen ill and they had come to pay their respects. What made the police think they had any right to intrude on a private party?

And although the Federal Bureau of Narcotics is certain that the private party was, in reality, a meeting of the Mafia Grand Council, today it is still far from proving it. Such is the veil of secrecy that surrounds the Mafia.

How can the Mafia continue to maintain its secrecy? Why, despite all our authority, despite all our reliable information, are we unequipped to cope with it? Mafia's secrecy is an ancient thing. According to legend, the organization was formed in Sicily during the Middle Ages. In those days, it was said to have worn a pious and a saintly face. True, it robbed the rich. But like Robin Hood it distributed its spoils among the poor. There are those who maintain that there was a time in the Mafia's history when it stretched out its hand to all of Sicily's poor people. They say it brought poetry and glamour into their lives. Many knowledgeable people, however, do not go along with the vagaries of such a legend. In their book, the Mafia was shrill and commercial almost from its beginning.

District Supervisor John T. Cusack of the Federal Bureau of Narcotics says:

"In its present form, the Mafia is generally considered to have been organized in Sicily during the late eighteenth century as a resistance to the Bourbon French conquest of the island but to have rapidly degenerated into a society of criminals."

It was not until the late nineteenth century that the menacing murmur of the Mafia first began to be heard in this country. In those days, it was known as the Black Hand, a reference to the trade-mark it stamped on its written threats. Its prime function was the exaction of tribute for what it chose to call "protection." It was a dim, dark mystery then, even more perfectly hidden than it is today. The numerous eerie murders it committed seemed to have no logical motivation, to have been accomplished out of no more than rage and phantasm.

Until 1920, the Mafia, for all its fierce fire, was a comparatively small-scale business. Prohibition launched it into the big time. Bootlegging was the bonanza which made possible later investments in every kind of business, legitimate as well as illegitimate.

Enforcement agencies today are depressed and bewildered by the Mafia's legitimate fronts. Too often they sniff the ominous Mafia scent in, say, the garment industry, and follow it to its source, only to discover that the men they hoped to identify as Mafiosi are seemingly eminent and respectable. No doubt about it: Mafia members, with the aid of their organization, are dominant in the olive oil, cheese, and export and import business. They control many of the wholesale fruit and produce markets of this country. They own hotels, motels, rooming houses, garment factories. They have infiltrated organized labor. They dominate the distribution of beer, liquor, and soft drinks and the vending-machine business, including cigarette machines and jukeboxes. They operate a host of restaurants, night clubs and bars. They hold interests in model and theatrical booking agencies and in the musical recording companies. Naturally all of their legitimate businesses serve to mask their illegitimate operations, notably the importation and distribution of narcotics.

How does Mafia do it? By means of ample money, deadly violence, and the use of "front people" who have no police records.

"Mafia members," says the Narcotics Bureau's John Cusack, "use 'front people' who are completely trusted, as the means to own and operate legitimate interests. By doing this they overcome licensing and income tax problems. Although legally in our courts of law, a 'front man,' or the ostensible owner of record, could eliminate the actual owner from these businesses, one would never do so, as this would bring certain death."

A review of the time-honored initiation ceremonies of Mafia gives some insight into its skeleton-shadowed omnipotence. Ceremonies are complete with oaths, the use of religious symbols and phrases, and primitive blood-lettings.

The Mafia oath reads, "I pledge my honor to be faithful to the Mafia, like the Mafia is faithful to me. As this saint and a few drops of my blood were burned, so will I give my blood for the Mafia, when the ashes and my blood will return to their original status."

Such sentiments, if a person believes in them, can make him feel an existence beyond himself. He can delude himself into thinking that, through his brothers of the past and the future, he is tasting a sort of immortality. Such a delusion is enough to make a man arrogant and impervious to authority. And, if this were not enough, there are the Mafia exhortations, springing from the view that these supermen are set above and apart from the rest of humanity.

Mafiosi must extend aid to brothers in distress and they must view an offense to one as an offense to all. Most important, they must never break the tradition of "omerta," silence. To Mafiosi, omerta means simply that if one reveals a secret of the organization he must die. But if he holds to the rules he will be rewarded by his fellow Mafiosi. Thus Mafiosi are taught various means by which they may communicate with one another when they are in a strange town and wish to make themselves known.

A question is asked of a likely stranger: "What time is it?"

If the stranger is a member of the clan he answers: "My watch is thirty minutes slow."

"Since when?"

"Since the twenty-fifth day of March, day of The Annunciation."

"Where were you on that day?"

"I was at (place where he was admitted to the society)."

"Who was there?"

"Lots of nice people."

"Whom do you adore?"

"The Annunciation of the Virgin Mary."

"What is your card?"

"Diamonds."

Back in the early days of the Mafia, its blood-and-death authoritarianism was gaudy and derisive to the authorities. Ignazio (Lupo the Wolf) Saietta, one of the first United States chieftains, ordered thirty-nine squealers slaughtered. They were shipped in trunks to fictitious addresses all over the country. Significantly, their tongues were slit.

The new Mafia no longer tolerates such clamorous doings. But the death of Big Al Anastasia proves that today, as yesterday, no Mafioso can afford to disdain the law of the organization. Indeed, the whole underworld which is at present allied with the Mafia fears its devil's blood.

The new Mafia was brought into being about twenty-five years ago by Charlie Lucky Luciano, then a lieutenant of the big boss, Joe Masseria. He believed that the competition between the club (the Mafia) and other mobs was dangerous. Clannishness was suicidal, he said. Why, since all the mobs had interlocking interests, did they try to kill each other off instead of seeking out ententes? He convinced three other top Mafiosi, Frank Costello, Joe Adonis and Willie Moretti, as well as his underworld allies, Meyer Lansky, Bugsy Siegel and Longie Zwillman, of the validity of his view.

But the older men of the Mafia, the revered Dons of the movement, could not understand Lucky's viewpoint. What was this talk about ententes with other mobs? And what made the young men think they were in any position to suggest policy for the organization? They were know-nothings. And yet here they were telling the older men, "Who cares about you? You're too old to live; go die, will you?" And the old men, horrified, unbelieving, said, "You talk like that to us, the grand Dons?" It was a convulsive, to-the-death schism between the generations.

The old men began to battle with the young ones. And the young ones didn't care. They decided that the old ones had to go.

The first old man to be killed was Masseria, the boss, on April 15, 1931. He was shot in the Coney Island restaurant of Gerardo Scarpato, where he had gone for a quiet dinner with Lucky, Joe Adonis and Albert Anastasia. Scarpato heard the gunfire in the kitchen and when he ran out he found the boss dead.

The other old men objected to Masseria's killing. But not too loudly. They knew that what had happened to him could also happen to them. They knew a revolution was on. And one night young disciples from all over the country held a meeting. The next morning there started a massacre that began in New York and avalanched all over the country. When it was over, thirty-five grand old Dons were ready for the undertaker's shroud. The young men were the bosses now. At a meeting of the Grand Council they elected Lucky Luciano to succeed Joe the Boss. Lucky remained in the position of boss of the Mafia until Special Prosecutor Thomas E. Dewey sent him to Sing Sing on sixty-two counts of compulsory prostitution. The same Mr. Dewey, as governor of New York, later paroled him and deported him to Italy for reasons that have never been adequately explained.

As soon as Lucky became boss he and his allies divided the underworld into separate syndicates—gambling, bookmaking, narcotics. Mafia men, looking out for its interests, were on the board of directors of every syndicate. So were the representatives of other powerful gangs, such as Meyer Lansky's and Bugsy Siegel's.

Although the Mafia has in a very real sense combined with other mobs, it still maintains its independence. Its prime administration is said to be in the hands of a ruling Don who is chosen in Palermo, Sicily, by a Grand Council made up of delegates from various countries. Until 1954, according to government sources, Don Calogero Vizzini was international head of the society. He was succeeded, after his death, by Don Giuseppe Russo. Rumor has it that Russo is also dead and that Lucky Luciano has taken over his post. Meanwhile Lucky's top deputy in this country is Vito Genovese.

Genovese is an old-time criminal. He skipped to fascist Italy in 1937 because he was wanted as a participant in the murder of gambler Ferdinand (The Shadow) Boccia. In Italy Genovese, with Mafia aid, took command of the black market and when the Allies during World War II came into Italy, he got a job as an army interpreter and craftily continued his black market operations. As a consequence of his black market activities, he came to the attention of the Army's Criminal

Investigation Division. Agent O. C. Dickey jailed him. Then Dickey learned that Genovese was wanted for murder back home.

But it seemed that nobody of any importance wanted to have anything to do with apprehending Genovese. For ten months Agent Dickey tried to get Genovese sent home for trial and was given the runaround by everyone he contacted. Finally he took matters into his own hands, escorted Vito to Brooklyn and turned him over to Assistant District Attorney Edward A. Heffernan.

Peter La Tempa, who was alleged to have witnessed the murder, was prepared to testify against Genovese. Knowing the workings of the Mafia, the authorities had La Tempa jailed for his own protection. Still, on the eve of the trial, he died in his cell and Judge Samuel Liebowitz had no alternative but to turn Genovese loose. Today, although he denies it, Genovese is reputed to be one of the largest narcotics importers in this country.

The Mafia's narcotics syndicate has front lines all over the world. Its organization is subtle and delicate. The big men of narcotics are sometimes worlds apart, often anonymous to one another, and yet they are so intermingled that together they comprise an implacable enemy. History reveals that the syndicate has survived any amount of bold, aggressive police sleuthing, not alone in this country, but also on the international scene.

In 1952 Charles Siragusa, a member of the Federal Narcotics Bureau's police system in Europe, discovered that most of the illegal heroin manufactured in Italy came from the plant of one of the country's most important pharmaceutical houses, Schiaperelli of Turin. Further investigation revealed that Carlo Migliardi, socially prominent top executive of the Schiaparelli Company, had secretly diverted about three hundred and fifty kilograms of heroin, worth some two million dollars, into this country. Migliardi's apprehension shocked Italy. The government immediately suspended the manufacture of heroin and enacted severe legislation against traders. It set up a police narcotics squad in Rome. Numerous arrests of Italian smugglers were effected. Lucky Luciano, known but not proved to be "the big man, the right man" of Italian narcotics smuggling, was confined to Naples and subjected to an 11 P.M. curfew. And yet Italy is today, as she was in 1952, a dominant source for the exportation of illegal drugs.

There is the story of the police and the cities of Marseilles, Paris and Le Havre. Two hundred leading Italian and French dealers who had been importing raw opium from the Middle East were rounded up in these cities and incarcerated. A triumphant France announced that Paris, Le Havre and Marseilles were through as narcotics export centers. But they are far from through.

And there is the Beirut story. In 1953, Agent Siragusa informed his boss, Harry Anslinger, Commissioner of the Federal Bureau of Narcotics, that most of the opium that was being converted into heroin and morphine in Europe appeared to be coming from Beirut. Anslinger ordered him and his men to apprehend the leaders of the Beirut mob. It was a difficult job because the Lebanese underworld exemplifies a curious solidarity between the legal and the illegal. It contains an uncountable number of taxi drivers, cafe waiters and hotel employees who have been hired to spy out and report on the doings of foreign interlopers. Still Siragusa was able to make contact with the head Beirut mobster, Abu Sayia.

Sayia had an elaborate organization that extended over Lebanon, Turkey, Syria and Greece. His principal associate was Ahment Ozisayer, a Turk who brought crude opium from the Turkish poppy-growers and smuggled it to Sayia's depots in Lebanon and Syria. From there the opium was shipped to Greece, France and Italy and thence around the rest of the world. The five countries concerned in Sayia's activities cooperated to break up his ring. Today, however, there is reputed to be a new and more powerful mob working out of Lebanon.

The international narcotics syndicate is not very different in its organizational setup from any large-scale business enterprise. To us in the United States, where a greater amount of illegal purchasing exists than anywhere else in the world, the importers, the sources of supply, are doubtless the most important men in the business although not necessarily the ones who make the most money. The importers buy drugs from the growers or their agents and smuggle it into this country. Each day numerous ships from foreign lands dock in our ports. Narcotics come in on the persons of merchant seamen and, sometimes, as part of the ships' cargoes. Airplanes handling overseas traffic also carry them. Both French and Italian agents get their crude opium from the poppy-growers in Turkey and, after manufacturing the heroin in illegal plants, bring it into New York. The Italians and the Frenchmen, "The Marseillers," are among the most powerful smuggling mobs, although Mexican gangs are beginning to run them a close second. In fact, one of the wealthiest mobs apprehended within recent years was the "La Nacha," working out of Mexico City. It grew its own poppies and manufactured its own heroin.

The narcotics distributors obtain their supply from the smugglers and distribute it to the wholesalers in various cities. There are no small-timers among them. They are usually disciplined mobs headed by top administrators, many of them Mafia-bred.

Paul B. Weston, former Inspector in the New York Police Department, says that "there are no fixed channels of distribution of narcotic drugs. For example, federal agents discovered a mob of distributors who took delivery from importers in North and South Carolina and sold the stuff to wholesalers in metropolitan New Jersey, while New Jersey distributors sought wholesale contacts in the Carolinas. . . . While the usual technique of the Carramusa mob was to smuggle narcotics across the border and to deliver it to buyers in Laredo and El Paso, they made deliveries far removed from the border—New York, San Francisco and even Seattle. . . . The Nuevo Laredo mob apparently supplied distributors all over the United States from California to New York."

The countrywide aspect of narcotics distribution was first brought to public light when Waxey Gordon was seized in New York. His apprehension triggered a total of twenty-three arrests of outlets in New Jersey, Illinois, New York, Missouri, Minnesota, Arizona, Nevada, Oregon and California. Gordon was the "source of supply." The others were his "outlets."

Possibly the most prosperous of the distributors are the "neighborhood mobs" of East Harlem. Despite any number of arrests of their so-called "chiefs," they endure through the years. Actually, since these groups are the most Mafia-oriented of any, the real masters never have been caught. Underlings, easily replaceable, have pretended to be the leaders and taken prison sentences. The most famous among the East Harlem mobs are said to be the 107th Streeters and the 116th Streeters.

Distributors sell only to wholesalers who are extremely well known to them and buy "big pieces" at a time, maybe ten, twenty, thirty kilos. Wholesalers never sell to users. To protect themselves against arrest, they sell only to carefully selected retailers who are not themselves addicted.

On the lowest plane of the drug-selling hierarchy are the small retailers, the peddlers. Prior to 1948, they worked alone, buying in one- and two-ounce lots and cutting their drugs only slightly. Their sales were only to addicts, although most of them were not addicted themselves. Since 1948, however, even peddling has become big business.

Inspector Weston says: "The mob [the peddling mob] is headed by one or two men and has from three to forty sellers, pushers and recruiters. The top man or two are not usually addicts but as we progress through the sellers, pushers, and recruiters, addiction rises. Almost all of the recruiters are addicts; and even the sellers have a fair proportion of addicts in their group."

To illustrate the connection between peddlers on different levels, Inspector Weston tells about some recent arrests in New York City.

A boss peddler was arrested on a rooftop in East Harlem. He was seized with a small scale, a box of empty capsules, a strainer, a quantity of milk sugar and several ounces of heroin. Police knew he was cutting a shipment from a wholesaler before making his contact with sellers.

A shooting-gallery proprietor, Vince, who sold shots for from two to five dollars, was arrested in his apartment. He was classified as a peddler, a subseller.

Dom bought one hundred fifty caps of heroin for sixty-two dollars from his boss, a seller. He peddled most of them for one dollar each, some for seventy-five cents, and a few he gave away to prospective customers—"Try it." He, of course, was a pusher.

Alice is an addict and a prostitute. She started another girl sniffing heroin and prostituting to pay for her habit. Alice also recruited her landlady's son to heroin. Each time she gets a new customer, her pusher gives her a break on her own price. If she brings enough "rookies" into "the fold," she'll be getting her own drug either for cost or gratis.

The boss peddler, the shooting-gallery proprietor, Dom and Alice belong to a mob in East Harlem. Their addict customers, exclusive of addict pushers and recruiters, total close to three hundred. They sell heroin, cocaine, "speedballs" which contain both these drugs and marijuana. Their prices vary from a top of five dollars for a jumbo capsule of heroin to a low of one dollar for three "Bams," weak marijuana cigarettes. Essentially businessmen and women, they cater to all types of customers, with a low-priced heroin cap at one dollar, a speedball cap at three dollars and "Dynamiters," extra-strong reefers, at one dollar each.

Other cities have similar sales mobs. Police recently uncovered a mob of twenty-one in Chicago and a mob of eighteen in Philadelphia. In New Orleans, where teen-age arrests doubled in 1950, several mobs of from seven to seventeen members were broken up. In Detroit, a mob of forty hung around places where high school students congregated and did a booming business.

Of course, we hear a great deal about "the deadly menace" of the selling gangs on the lowest rungs of the hierarchical ladder. We hear a lot about the "victims of the pushers and recruiters." And when one small mob or another is broken up by police action, we get the comfortable feeling that "something is being done." But we do not realize that so long as there is addiction in this country, small-time sellers are bound to remain chronic evils. It is naïve to assume that there is not a new small-timer to replace anyone who gets arrested. Actually, the pushers and recruiters are tools of the big smugglers, distributors and wholesalers, just as the addicts are. The smugglers, distributors and wholesalers are the ones who keep the narcotics traffic flourishing. To date, they are beyond the control and even the ken of the police.

Chapter **2**   **Portrait Of A Young Hood**

One of the principal wholesalers in Junktown, U.S.A., is Joe Barbetta, present chieftain of the 116th Streeters, probably the wealthiest neighborhood "club" associated with the narcotics syndicate. Joe Barbetta is better known in his neighborhood as Joe Babes or Joe the Baby.

He was born in Italy of a respectable family. His father, Giovanni, was a fine, big man with a walrus mustache. His mother, Lucia, was a sweet and gentle woman, with dark doe's eyes, always dressed in a long, loose, ill-fitting black dress.

Back home during the years before he had come to America, Giovanni had been known as the paisan with the thunderous voice. But life in America toned him down. He who had never been timorous in his life suddenly grew faint-hearted in the face of the construction bosses for whom he worked. He worked hard, for he had a great dream, security for his children. Someday, they would live in houses with steam heat. They would wear fine clothes and people would lift their hats to them as they walked down the street.

And then, one day, Giovanni's bosses laid him off. His whole life cracked open. He did not know how to handle himself as an unemployed man. His hands began to shake and he cried around the house. To his children, he said:

"I did you pain when I brought you here. Would that I were never born."

"No, Papa. Do not talk so."

But they could not comfort him. He felt as though he had committed a crime toward them. This was Giovanni the papa.

And Lucia, the mama, still mourned the two daughters she lost a year before the family had embarked for America. Mother in heaven, it was always somebody dying. Make your peace. But Lucia could not do that. She was a pessimist. She was certain that her whole family would soon be marching to the poorhouse.

"My pigeon," she would say to Joe, "the promises I made to you will never come true."

Joe would answer, *"I* will make the promises come true."

But living in that house with a heart-sick father and mother and five brothers and sisters, it did not seem likely that the promises *could* ever come true.

Of course Joe never spent much time around the house. East 116th Street was like a magnet to him from the time he was eight years old. His street. His neighborhood. It was not just a bunch of houses in Joe's book. It was the crossroads of the universe. Anything could happen there and usually did. Weddings. Funerals. Card games with the tables set up outside the houses. Arguments over political matters. Soapbox speeches. Fistfights. Fiestas.

When Joe walked down 116th Street, he never knew whom he would meet. There were the good priests. There were the elderly men and women who hogged the sidewalks next to their houses. Day after day, they would sit on their campstools talking of this and that. The old women would always greet Joe lovingly:

"Good going, little pigeon."

And there were the Mafiosi, the Black Handers. The Mafia during the years when Joe Barbetta was growing up did not rake in the more than three billion dollars it does today, but it was still a well-organized crime cartel. It was then, as it is today, no ordinary gang, held loosely together by greed and terror. The greed and terror were there, all right, but they were rigidly controlled and, most important, hidden under a cloak of fraternalism. When Joe was little, the local Dons of the Mafia, for all their wealth, were neighbors who would stop and chat with him. Still and all, they seemed kings of the universe. They were men who asked no favors from anyone and were finished with the brute scramble in which Joe's father was still pitiably engaged.

No wonder Joe aped them. He organized his own gang and began strutting the way the Mafiosi did. He and the other boys robbed candy and dime stores for the sport. They played hooky from school. They were tough and game as they come. It took just a whispered "Wop" or "Eytie bastard" to make them put up their fists and fight.

Joe was always something special with the Mafiosi. They nicknamed him the baby, Joe the Baby. "That little Joe," they would tell one another, "that baby, did you see him lift his little fists and fight?" They liked him because he was such a strong child. And he grew stronger as he grew older. By the time he was fifteen years old, he and the boys he led stopped being just restless and roving and out for sport. They were still restless and roving, certainly, but they were also purposeful as could be. The money was what they wanted now.

When Joe was seventeen years old he took his first bust. He was arrested on a burglary job. The three boys who worked with him got away. Joe would not reveal their identities. It was said around the neighborhood that the police struck him with their fists until his face was numb and that still he would not talk. All over, wherever men lounged, in the candy stores, in the poolrooms, Joe's friends told his story.

"That Joe's O.K. The cops slap him around. They kick his teeth in. They hit him over the head. And he never opens his yap. He tells them, 'What do you want from me? I didn't do nothing. I don't know nothing. You're killing me. I got a heart attack.' He don't open up. He's the hardest to crack ever."

Joe was sent to jail. The 116th Streeters heard many reports of his activities there. It was said that he and his supporters got hold of the weak ones in the prison and took away the money they had on them. Then they bought off the guards. They walked free while the other prisoners stayed in their cells.

By the time Joe came out on the street again, he was nineteen years old and had acquired a reputation that awed members of his old gang.

"Hey, you just got done with your bit, huh?"

"Yeah."

"How'd you do it?"

"On my ear. What do you mean, how'd I do it? You make up your mind and you do it."

And the talk about Joe continued. "He's a good kid. He plays the game. He gets dropped. He takes a bit. He doesn't suffer about it. He doesn't cry about it. He never opens up. He can go places."

After Joe had been out of jail for a couple of weeks, he was contacted by bullet-headed Johnny Pagano in behalf of "the club." Everybody on 116th Street knew "the club, the organization." It was also known as "the family." Its head-quarters served as the center of operations for the local Mafia. Its membership ran the gamut all the way from the grand leaders to the hopeful novices drawn out of the kid gangs.

Johnny said, "Now you done your bit, Joe, what you going to do?"

"Well, I don't know yet."

"Oh look, you got to do a little business. There is no sense in your walking around like this. Got anything on for tomorrow night?"

"Who me? No, nothing."

"Well, I'll tell you what you do. Come around the club tomorrow about seven o'clock."

"What for?"

"Hey, what's the matter? You asking questions?"

"No. No. I'll be there O.K."

The club was a gloomy cellar apartment. It contained a couple of couches and chairs and there was an excuse for a desk sitting in the middle of the floor. But to Joe, the club, for all its scrimy, motheaten quality, was as glamorous as the Hotel Ritz. He was exultant at the thought of being there. Some of the big men were sitting around in shirt sleeves and suspenders. They were not the very big men, of course, not the top leaders. But, they were high-riding all the same. The famous Joey Mattino, scowling and evil, was smoking a cigar and leaning his hands on the desk. He acted as though he considered Joe Babes his equal. After a while, he said:

"Kid, you know Eddie Boy Mancuso from down the

block? He's got too big for his breeches. I want you and Salvatore Lucania, Salvatore from 14th Street, to go down and take care of him for me. Hey, you know Salvatore from 14th Street?"

Certainly Joe knew Salvatore from 14th Street. He was short and puny, but fearless. He said, "Yes sir, I know Salvatore from 14th Street."

"Well, like I said, you and Salvatore take care of Eddie Boy for me. He's to get a small beating, a small beating, not too much now, just a little beating so he'll know we are not happy."

That night Joe and Salvatore went to where Eddie Boy lived. They broke a couple of his ribs. Someone who witnessed the beating called the police. But when they arrived, Eddie Boy refused to answer their questions.

"I tell you I don't know who hit me. I never seen the guys before. These two fellows here? They're my best friends. They was visiting me. What do you mean, why didn't they stop the fight? What could they do? This wasn't none of their business. Charges? What do you mean, charges? Who the hell you going to charge anyways? Forget it, boys, forget it."

Eddie Boy was taken to the hospital after the officers left. And Joe and Salvatore went to Joe's house and played some records. They became confidential with one another and as they talked, it came out that they both had the gangman's off-beat perspective on the world. You have, somehow, to make the big time; how you do it does not matter.

A couple of nights after Eddie was beaten, Joe was again summoned to the club and Joey Mattino told him:

"Listen, Baby, the neighborhood. Things is going to pot. We got to get organized, you know?" He gave him a list of bars and grills that had been paying revenue to the Mafia for many years. He said, "Baby, I want you should get ahold of these punks and tell them: 'You are not doing right by the area here. You are not doing right by the neighborhood. It ain't safe if you don't give them another ten bucks a week.' "

Joe went around to the bars and grills and told the owners:

"You got to contribute ten dollars more a week to the neighborhood club. You know yourself you got to have a club. If you don't have club, guys are going to have nothing to do. So they'll come to the bars and they'll drink. They're going to get high and then you get trouble and you don't want trouble. Give them a club. Let the bums go to a club."

The smart saloonkeepers were easy for Joe to handle. They were aware of the treatment they might expect if they did not meet the Mafia's request. But a few men, either too small-time and dazzled by the dollar or too individualistic, voiced their objections:

"Gee, Baby, I can't afford another ten."

"Listen, I'm your friend. You better afford it. Still, it's up to you. I don't want to tell nobody what to do. You got to make up your own mind. I'll come back in a couple of days to get your answer."

At the end, there was only one young man who wouldn't pay the extra ten dollars, Pallechia, who had inherited his bar from his father.

"No good, fellow, I don't want to be shaken down no more than I been already."

That night Joe and some other young members of the club went touring the bars. By the time they reached Pallechia's place they were drunk and rambunctious. Somebody tried to pick a fight with Joe and it was natural that his friends would take a stand behind him. Who was to blame that the bar got damaged, and that the Alcoholic Beverage Control Board took Pallechia's liquor license away because there had been a riot in his place?

Good boy. Good Joe. He's shaping up fine. He's mastering the vital foundations of club work. He does everything he's asked, even filthy, little jobs, and he's always relaxed, always gracious.

Over the years, the police had caught Joe up on a few of the jobs he'd done for the Mafia. But he handled the officers with sureness. His nerves were never on edge. He was never jittery. He could take anything. He always gave the cops one answer: *"I don't know nothing."* He was solid. He was "a stand-up boy." And, when he got back home after serving a sentence, he never talked about what had gone on in jail. Everyone agreed that he was good Mafia material, young but properly disciplined. He was waiting to get into the big time but he trusted the right men to know when he was ready to be promoted. In the meantime he acted satisfied with whatever assignments they gave him.

Joe was satisfied. After all, he had plenty of money during the hard years of the Depression. He dressed his sisters in high style. He backed his father in a tailoring shop. He bought his mother many presents. She often boasted about him. Joe felt himself a great man when he was with his mother. Of course he wondered once in a while whether she knew how he was making his money. Not that he was disturbed or ashamed over what he was doing. He figured that a man had to be sharp in order to take care of his family. And now, providing for his family was a big job for Joe, for he had a new wife, Rita, and a son, Luigi. They must never want for anything.

The Mafia hierarchy, unknown to Joe the Baby, watched him develop and grow. The middle-men who supervised him gave the big men periodic reports on him. That's the way it is with a promising punk in the organization. Everyone keeps an eye on him. How does he do the picayune tasks he's been assigned? Has he really lived up to the high hopes people had when they became acquainted with him? After all, a mobster is different from a kid-gang leader, no matter how bright and brave. How has this one assimilated the theory of the mob? Is he quick? How does he react under pressure? Bring him up slowly and find out everything there is to know about him. The Mafia, like any business organization, is hungry for good men. But they must be trustworthy. A Mafia man always knows that he is considered reliable when he is invited into the back room of the club. An invitation into the back room is the greatest experience in the life of any young Mafia punk. It signifies that a new hood, a new star of mobsterdom, is about to be born. It means the punk is about to be let in on the secret of the right man who occupies a master's seat in the family and whom the vast majority of the membership cannot identify.

On what he still considers the greatest day of his life, Joe Babes was invited by Johnny Pagano into the back room. When he saw the man in the master's chair Joe could hardly believe his eyes—the man was Salvatore Lucania from 14th Street, the same Salvatore who had accompanied him on his first Mafia assignment. Salvatore was changed, though. He had a new name, Charlie Lucky Luciano and a new hard crust. The old Dons bowed and smiled when he spoke. He turned out to be the favorite lieutenant of Joe Masseria, Mafia's big boss. He told Joe Babes:

"Baby, I remember you from way back. I like you. I got a job for you. Later, the boys'll introduce you to a girl called Ann. Tomorrow night she's going to go walking down 109th Street with a guy. You'll pick them up on Second Avenue and follow them. When Ann takes out her handkerchief you'll give the guy a hit, a good hit; kill him."

Tomorrow night came. Joe stood on the corner of 109th Street and Second Avenue. And now, here came Ann with the man, laughing and strolling slowly. Ann held the man's arm. Joe followed them for a block and a half before Ann dropped her handkerchief. He pulled his gun out of his own handkerchief. One shot, and the man, whoever he was, was dead. There was a black Cadillac waiting for Joe the Baby. He was driven to New Rochelle and told to take the train home from there.

To do a killing on assignment is a mob punk's biggest chance to connect with the right men. Joe Babes connected with Charlie Lucky Luciano. From the beginning he had an instinct that Lucky, rather than any of the old Dons, was the man to follow. Lucky repaid his faith. He made him his personal bodyguard. And after the massacre of the old Dons, which included the 116th Street chieftain, he made Joe the big boss of the 116th Street territory. The boss of a territory gets his cut on all neighborhood enterprises—the crap games, the shakedowns, the gambling, the goon-organizing, and the narcotics. Joe knew what to do with his money when he got it. He saved it and invested it all in narcotics.

Chapter 3 Old Yard-Dog

Charlie Lucky put Joe in touch with the right men of the narcotics syndicate. They agreed to introduce him to important smugglers. And they instructed him about the best methods of conducting the business. They told him that the most important element in avoiding police interference was a man's choice of his number-one assistant, his plant manager. The plant manager, after all, is the right man's active administrator. In a sense, he is in charge of the whole business. He supervises the places where the narcotics are cut and stashed and packaged, made ready for distribution to the big buyers. He also directs the runners who deliver the prepared narcotics to the wholesalers. It is said in gangland that a plant manager "can make or break a junk man. He's got to be hip to people, smart. At the same time, he's got to think he's a mug without his junker. He's got to have a little of the old yard-dog in him."

Joe Babes found himself the ideal manager, Mimi Marrano. He had known Mimi since they had both been small children. Mimi had been a short, fat boy who wobbled when he walked. He had a mop of black hair he never combed. The other children teased him. They called him baby elephant, "Belly" for short.

"Hey, Belly, what's the matter? Don't your mother feed you good? You're getting skinny."

"Belly, you're wasting away to a ton, you know that?"

Mimi raved when the kids called him Belly. But they didn't care. They grinned and went on harassing him.

One day, out of some kind of peculiar paternal instinct, Joe the Baby yelled at the ones who taunted Mimi.

"Listen, you leave Mimi alone."

"Yeah? What for?"

"Because I say so."

"Baby, what's it to you? What you taking up for Belly for?"

"It's my business."

It took a couple of months, but finally the other boys knew that Mimi was Joe's personal property. They knew that unless they wanted to tangle with Joe, they had better leave Mimi alone.

No wonder Mimi is so devoted to Joe today. When a man grows up the way Mimi did, he develops strong loyalties. When he likes a man, he loves him. He is ready to do anything in the world for him.

As much as Mimi loves Joe Babes, that's how much he hates other people. When he was little, all he wanted was peace. But now he wants revenge for the indignities he experienced as a child. He has grown more stunted as he has grown older. But he has learned not to let his feelings show. He has learned how to play the traditional role of the fat boy. He acts jovial. And, although everyone but Joe is a leper to him in reality, he behaves as though he has a great love for humanity.

Only once in a while he allows his true hostility to seep out. One afternoon, while he was telling jokes to his friends, another small, fat man, Dominic Pasta, came along and started to tell some of his own jokes.

"Dominic," Mimi said, "get the hell off this corner. Disappear."

"How come you tell me to disappear? You own this corner? Maybe you own Brooklyn Bridge too. Maybe you could get kind and let me acrost it sometimes."

"I could get real kind, Dominic," Mimi said, "if I seen you dying. You just got to show me you're dying and I'll get *real* kind."

"Oh, I'm laughing," Dominic held his hand on his stomach. "Hey, comedian!"

"You're not laughing now." Mimi said. "Maybe you'll laugh later, then."

That night, Mimi and a couple of his men routed Dominic out of bed. They forced him to serve them his best liquor.

"You call this whiskey, man?" Mimi asked. "Why, this ain't got no more kick than chocolate malted has."

What happened later is still talked of along 116th Street.

"Stand Dominic up," Mimi told his two friends. "Hold the bastard against the wall."

He slapped him. He spat into his face. He urinated on him.

When Mimi first began working for Joe he looked for a perfect plant for stashing the heroin. He wanted a "cop-proof dommy," a place where, one way or another, he could be informed of any raiding police officers before they reached him. He found the ideal apartment; three and a half rooms of a divided railroad flat on the third floor of a five-story tenement. It faced on the fire escape at the front of the building. Mimi's men occupied several of the other apartments, both front and back. He would therefore be bound to be informed in the event of a police assault. His friends talk, with great gusto, about many unsuccessful police raids on Mimi's plant.

"The coppers come prowling around and somebody tosses Mimi the hint. So next thing you know he swoops up all his junk and flushes it down the toilet. By the time them coppers got his door kicked down, he and his dommy are both clean as whistles. 'Hey, what's the matter?' he says. 'Where'd you leave your manners at? Next time, knock.' "

After he had found Joe the perfect plant, Mimi located a fine old couple to live in it and give it a look of legality. Ma and Pa Carano are good, clean-living people. Pa is sixty-nine years old, Ma sixty-seven. They go to church every Sunday.

Ma and Pa Carano had one daughter and three sons. Two of the sons are dead. The eldest, Anthony, died in the last war. He was a hero. Ma and Pa have all his medals. They keep them enshrined in their china closet. There is always a light burning over those medals. No matter how poor they get, they'll keep that light burning. The light comes first. It comes before eating.

The second son, Vito—Willie, they called him in the neighborhood—went to Chicago. A big, healthy, strapping boy and he goes away and dies and his parents never know how or why.

Angelina, the daughter, is married to a decent, upstanding man. But he is poor as the Sicilian hillside. And already there are six children to be clothed and fed.

Salvatore, the baby, is in jail. A child and still he must wake up every morning behind prison walls. If his parents had their way they would be in that prison and he would be at home.

Salvatore's wife Nancy goes with men for money.

One day, when he could not contain himself any longer, Pa Carano spoke to Salvatore's wife. He could not keep from crying.

"Nancy, you're my son's wife. I want to call you daughter."

She looked at him contemptuously. "What are you crying for? Can't you look at me without crying? You must hate me plenty."

"Nancy, daughter, I must call you daughter, it's you I weep for. Everything hurts me when I know what you do."

She laughed in his face. "Listen, old man, I got to live, don't I?"

Mimi came along when life looked bleakest for the Caranos. He gave them a nice apartment, rent-free, gas, electricity and telephone all paid for, and one hundred fifty dollars a month besides. One hundred fifty dollars plus social security was big money in their eyes. Two old people, how much money do they need when their rent is all paid? They eat like birds. And besides, mama's a good cook; she can do more with cheap cuts of meat than other women can with expensive ones. So they take some of Mimi's money and help Angelina out of her trouble. And what's left over from Angelina, they can give to Nancy. Maybe she'll stop her streetwalking then.

Ma and Pa Carano are not unconscious of the role they are playing for Mimi and Joe the Baby. They are fully aware of the fact that they can be arrested any day. But they are old mother hens working for their chicks. What wouldn't they do for the children?

Mimi chooses his runners as carefully as his stash-sitters. He wants sturdy, solid boys, young Joe Babes in the making.

Today he has three nineteen-year-olds working under him. When they first began, he told them:

"Look, you guys, stay around all the time, 'cause if I need you, I want you. Don't fool around. Stay right here by the club and I will call you."

So they hang around the club all night on the chance that Mimi will have an errand for them. Some nights they have nothing to do. Other nights there is no time to rest.

"You, kid, go to 457 East 115th Street. Lay this under the radiator. Hole up until somebody picks up on it."

"Hey, you. Come here. Load this in the garbage can outside of 313. Wait around."

"Now, what I want you to do, kid, throw this in the Ford with the Jersey license on 112th. Eye the guy that gets it."

Mimi pays his runners twenty-five dollars for each delivery. It does not matter whether the runner delivers five ounces or five kilos. The pay is the same and so is the sentence a runner is likely to get if he is caught. In New York, to be found with more than one eighth of an ounce containing one per cent or more of heroin automatically makes a person a felon. And therefore the straight twenty-five dollars per delivery.

"Lousy money?" Mimi says. "Maybe. But listen, cat, that's the way of the play. You got to take it or leave it, Jack."

His runners are happy to take whatever he offers. They are not working for money alone. Mimi's is the drilling academy they must graduate from before they can amount to anything with the 116th Streeters. Mimi has told them that the rewards of their jobs more than make up for the risks.

"Look, kid," he says, "what's the worst can happen to you? You get collared. The coppers play you sweet at first. They tell you they know the stuff ain't yours and you're a nice kid. They say, 'Just tell us who the man is and you can go home.' Well, you ain't going to tell them about me. So you say, 'There's no man. I'm the man. The stuff's mine.' Well, after a while they smack you around. They try to make you blow your top. You don't blow it. O.K. So you got a rap coming up. You get five, seven, ten years. So, how old'll you be when you come out of the pen? Twenty-four, twenty-six, twenty-nine? Still young. And you're my boys. I will give you two kilos of pure because you didn't lay down cold on me."

So no matter what the coppers do, Mimi's runners will hold their own. They'll never be broken. They're like Joe was twenty years ago. They're still singing his theme song:

"Listen, what do you want from my life? *I don't know nothing about nobody.*"

This is what makes the Mafia endure. Omerta. Keep your mouth shut and you live. Talk and you die. Mimi's kids know that if the coppers catch them they'll be wise to take their bits without complaining. And when they come out of jail, they'll start with two kilos of pure heroin.

Two kilos of pure. Mimi's boys cut it in half. Now they have four kilos of fifty per cent pure. The merchandise is worth at least forty thousand dollars. They put the money they make on it back in the business. They soon grow rich. They feel fortunate to have had an opportunity to have gone to jail for Mimi.

In a sense, of course, Mimi's boys have no choice. They cannot save themselves from prison sentences by informing on him. They, too, have been brought up on the code of omerta. They know that they will be killed if they ever tell on Mimi or anyone else in "the family."

Giacomo Marconi once told on a "family man." He was one of Mimi's distributors, a man of forty-five. About four years ago, he was picked up for third-offense trafficking. A third offense means at least fifteen years behind bars. Giacomo was forty-five, not nineteen. He would be sixty years old before he'd get out of jail. How much of life would be left to him then? So when the police promised him immunity if he would act as their stool pigeon, he whimpered out the names of a couple of men who were lower in the hierarchy than he was himself. After he told his story and was released, he went to a Turkish bath, hoping that he could build his time there into an alibi if anyone asked where he had been.

But the 116th Streeters, like the larger Mafia, have seasoned spies in police circles. They know when one of their own turns into a stool pigeon, no matter how he tries to screen his activity, and they conduct a regular court to determine his innocence or guilt. Joe Babes served as judge in Marconi's trial, held the night after the police had picked him up.

"All right," Joe asked, "where were you last night?"

"Down by the Turkish bath."

"Which one?"

"46th Street. I don't know. I think 46th Street."

"Anyone see you there?"

"I don't know. Jeez, Joe."

"Where were you before you went to the Turkish bath?"

"In my room."

"What were you doing there?"

"Sleeping."

"Suppose I tell you you were not in your room."

"I was."

"Suppose I tell you you were dropped. Suppose I tell you the coppers had you?"

"What do you mean? I wasn't dropped. Honest. I swear on my mother's grave."

"All right," Joe said, "call Melvin."

Melvin is a teen-ager from West Harlem. He has contact with many officers. The moment Marconi saw Melvin, he told the truth.

"Yeah, Joe, I was dropped."

As the story is told around, Joe told Giacomo Marconi to go home and live, but to be careful. And then, it is said that Mimi told Joe he thought he'd been misled by his generosity into making a mistake, that it was dangerous to let Giacomo live. And Joe said, all right, let him die then. The next morning Giacomo was found dead on the floor of his furnished room.

Mimi said that he didn't like to advise Joe to have Giacomo killed, but that the 11th Streeters could not afford to permit a known stool pigeon to go on living in their midst.

Mimi's word is law along 116th Street because he speaks for Joe. Besides, he's a sixty–seventy-thousand-dollar-a-year man. Even if he does look like a ragpicker. Oh, yes, he's still got the uncombed hair. He's still as round as he is tall.

Those who know the mob best say not to worry about Mimi. Give him ten years and a couple of good lieutenants and you'll see some changes. He'll improve himself if he decides to. He'll stop talking through the corner of his mouth. He'll acquire new knowledge, new taste. He'll get good clothes and learn how to wear them. And then, if he wants to, he'll mix with legitimate millionaires.

Impossible? Stranger things have happened. Take the case of Frank Costello as one example. He's known to be a sportsman and intimate of blue bloods. One day, according to the grapevine again, Costello was at the racetrack. He sat in the box of one of the wealthiest men in the country and he told the millionaire he figured his horse would lose the race.

He said, "I'll bet you fifty your horse can't win."

The horse did win and Costello handed the millionaire fifty thousand dollars. The millionaire said, "but the bet was for fifty dollars, not fifty thousand."

"My bet was for fifty thousand."

"But if you had won, I would have given you fifty."

"That's because you understood the bet to be for fifty. I understood it to be for fifty thousand. When I say fifty, I mean fifty thousand. If I had meant fifty dollars I would have said five-o."

If Frank Costello could make the big time, who is to say Mimi cannot? But as they say along East 116th Street:

"A cat's got to be plenty sick of his own life to go out and try to make the squares."

Maybe Frank Costello and Lucky Luciano were sickened by the same misfortune. Lucky always used to say, "I'd rather die than be a punk." He could never forget his slum-shocked childhood.

Of course most mobsters wouldn't dream of leaving the world in which they grew up. They are afraid. And so they convince themselves that they do not care about the "square" world. They say, "To hell with the righteous gees who make with the pretty talk. Me, I don't have to talk pretty through my mouth. My *fists* talk pretty. Besides, money talks—loud."

These mobsters are glad they look tough.

"Listen," they say, "I don't need to tog sharp unless I want to, see? And I don't need to start learning nothing I don't know now."

Joe Priori is one who says that. He is only twenty-two years old and yet he is a big seller along 116th Street. He has his own selling gang of some fourteen people and he handles forty to fifty thousand dollars a week. He can lose twenty-five thousand dollars in a crap game with no crying, no regrets. Priori's a big, clumsy-looking boy who can hardly read or write.

"So what?" he asks. "All right, so I couldn't learn my a-b-c's in school. Them teachers called me a moron 'cause I wasn't no good at reading and writing. Who's the moron now? How much money they got in their jeans, I like to know. I don't need to read. What's to read? Only the sports in the *Daily News*. I can do it. Listen, I got so much bread I could hire a gang of them teachers to read me the sports news. They better read right too. They better read good. Them teachers don't know I can add figures in my head. It's more'n they can do theirselves."

Of course, the right men encourage boys like Priori to stay simple. Their simplicity makes them ideal for taking orders. There is no competitiveness in them.

"Hey, Priori," Joe Babes asks during the rare times he comes to the club these days. "You happy, kid?"

"Yeah," Priori says, "sure."

Many mobsters maintain that the Prioris are lucky. They say it is not easy to figure out the secrets of the well-born people, not easy to learn ways they should have been taught when they were children.

Dale Carnegie is not just a name in the underworld. It's a symbol. How to make friends and influence people. Respect yourself. Stand up straight and look the world in the eye. Learn how to speak properly. Don't say "dese" or "dose." Caress your vowels. *Aaa, eee, ooo, uuu*. Go to Arthur Murray's classes, learn the cha-cha. Learn the hot-cha-cha. You must start working with a tailor too as soon as you hit the big money. He's the one to define your style.

A few mobsters, intense in their search for the "square" values, spend years figuring them out. Joe Babes is one who acquired them. Twenty years ago he was a sort of Mimi, although taller, more slender and better looking. But he dressed badly and talked poorly. He went out with semi-prostitutes, clotheshorses, glamorous maybe but available to any man for the price of a mink stole or even a hat with a Paris label. Joe soon tired of those women and of the whole sporting world. He decided to get in tune for the "square big time."

Today, Joe Babes looks like an established banker. He is a conservative dresser who always wears dark, perfectly fitted suits and muted ties. His hair is graying at the temples. He affects horn-rimmed glasses. He looks very distinguished, more or less.

Like the legimate businessman he claims to be. Joe Babes in narcotics? Never. Not in narcotics and not in prostitution. And if you think for a moment that Joe is in narcotics, prove it. He is "not the most moral man in the world," but then neither is he "the most immoral."

"For instance," he says in a quiet voice, slightly New England in intonation, "I do gamble now and then. I can't help it. It's a disease. It's in my blood. But junk? Never. I'd die first. Listen, I grew up in a neighborhood where slews of young people were destroyed by junk. I hate the men who deal in such sickening stuff."

Joe owns a small factory, the Barbetta Tool and Dye Works. He owns stock in one of the principal liquor distilleries. And he owns a couple of strip joints in Greenwich Village. He also angels Broadway shows. Nowadays he escorts up-and-coming starlets around to the best places. They're lovely girls, charming, artistic, fashionable but not flashy.

As for his wife and children, he keeps them in a beautiful, ten-room house on Long Island. Like all hoods' wives, Rita does not try to impose her standards on Joe. She knows she must be flexible. Not that Joe would divorce her if she were not. A divorced wife might go to the police. Besides, oddly but truly, it is a rare hood who would divorce "the mother of my sons." Of course, divorce is not the only way to control women. Irritating wives have been known to get "hits in the head," and their murderers have usually remained anonymous.

Rita has her children. She has her home. And she wears beautiful clothes. Joe feels he is a good husband. He is certainly a proud and doting father.

Joe Babes, according to his neighbors, is a generous man. He gives thousands of dollars to charity every year. He chairs the trustee boards of some very legitimate welfare organizations.

Many big mobsters make outstanding contributions to charity. These include Frank Costello, Vito Genovese and the equally important, if less well-known Fred C. Delvi. Fred Delvi is a one-man movement for aiding the homeless and the downtrodden. He works for Korean war orphans, Greek mothers, Negro college students, Polish refugees, Russian emigrés.

And yet those who know Fred C. best say there was a time, not too long ago, when he was merely another 116th Street punk. His admirers say that he was a Golden Gloves champion at sixteen and that the big Dons of the Mafia began using him as a stone-hitter when he was still in his teens. He is rumored to have been responsible for some of the biggest mob killings in recent years. Even money has it that when Bugsy Siegel of Los Angeles was killed, Fred C. organized the murder.

And yet the police cannot arrest Fred. "We know all about his doings," they say. "At least we suspect what they are. But the man is no more than a shadow to us. We have reason to suppose that he is as highly placed in the Mafia as Vito Genovese, perhaps more highly placed, but we haven't got a bat's chance of proving it."

Fred C. lives elegantly in Cuba and was an intimate of ex-dictator Fulgencio Batista. In his own private plane he flies back and forth between Cuba, the U.S. and Europe. Although police know that his vast income is made through the importation of narcotics, he denies it. Like Joe Babes, he claims to be a legitimate businessman who gambles on the side to relieve his pressure. He socializes with many U.S. governors whose states maintain racetracks, and with senators and congressmen. He has helped support more than one presidential campaign.

What are we going to do about the Fred C. Delvis, the so-called legitimate businessmen of narcotics? And what are we going to do about our addicts?

BOOK III

Addiction
and
The Law

1 "The Army Navy And Marine Corps—"

Law-enforcement officers differ widely as to the best methods of controlling addiction. Some favor intensified international control. They say that addiction could be combatted once and for all if the world supply of narcotics were restricted to the amounts known to be needed for medicinal and research purposes. Many American experts, however, reject international control as unworkable and maintain that we, ourselves, must take responsibility for introducing more severe national and local control in this country. Actually, all these suggested controls are being utilized today, as effectively as possible under the circumstances. There is global control of narcotics growth, manufacture and distribution. There is national control of illicit traffic within the United States, resting with the Bureau of Narcotics of the U.S. Treasury Department. And there is local control as effected by city police departments. In addition, the U.S. Customs Bureau has the job of keeping illicit narcotics from being smuggled into our seaports and across our boundaries.

Since 1912, efforts at universal limitation have been made through international compacts, through the League of Nations, and—more recently—through the United Nations, which has two agencies devoted to the regulation of lawful international traffic in narcotics and the suppression of illicit traffic. The Permanent Central Opium Board of the U.N. attempts to determine the legitimate medical and research needs for opium and its derivatives throughout the world, while the U.N. Commission on Narcotic Drugs, an agency of the Economic and Social Council, tries to keep a check on the illicit traffic of these drugs and to draw up and enforce international control measures.

Several years ago the Commission drafted a global agreement according to which all narcotic-producing, manufacturing and consuming nations would undertake to limit the flow and use of such drugs to legitimate channels. But they were unable to achieve agreement. The affected nations were too different in their points of view. Some countries see no need for laws against selling and using narcotics. Some lands have laws, and yet their customs are such that opium smoking and eating must be tolerated. And in countries in South America which produce cocaine, chewing coca leaves is more or less commonplace. So long as there are so many differences among countries, can we expect that any effort at world control will be successful?

The Permanent Central Opium Board of the United Nations has stated that:

"The most effective regulations are powerless to control the international traffic unless they are fully carried out by governments in their national control and in their cooperation with other governments."

The Board estimates that well over two thousand tons of opium are produced annually, whereas the amount needed for legitimate medicinal and research purposes throughout the world totals only about four hundred fifty tons a year. Until recently, countries such as Italy, Turkey and Greece manufactured many times more than the amounts of morphine and heroin needed for domestic consumption or legitimate export.

These three countries are now limiting their manufacture. But it seems that, as one country is closed off as a source, another one takes its place. During the years of World War II, China, Yugoslavia and Italy could not be used, as they had been previously, as sources of opium supply. But U.S. distributors were not troubled. They merely made contact with smugglers from the ports of Great Britain, Iran and India. Similarly, when normal channels of sea and air commerce were closed, Mexico made its appearance as a great source of U.S. supply. It was estimated that in 1943 two thirds of our prepared opium was of Mexican origin.

While the United Nations has managed to effect some areas of international agreement and also to stimulate individual nations to a sense of responsibility, we must still face the fact that the illicit traffic increases year by year. It is doubtful whether, even if the U.N. achieved its hope for a U.N.-controlled monopoly of the world opium trade (commercial and political issues have made this impossible so far), the unlawful operators could be stopped from their smuggling and distributing.

If international narcotics control is basically ineffective, what about national control? Has the U.S. Customs Bureau been able to keep the smugglers out of our seaports? Of course not. The whole concept is unrealistic. How can a single enforcement unit, consisting of fewer than two hundred fifty customs agents, be expected to suppress the traffic in an area of three million square miles with almost five thousand miles of coastline? Actually, of course, it would not matter if the force were quadrupled. It still could not make a dent in the mobsters' activities. Harry Anslinger, U.S. Commissioner of Narcotics, once said that the entire United States Army, Navy and Marine Corps could not keep narcotics out of New York City. This is due not alone to geography and to the ingenuity of the smugglers, but also to the well-known fact that mobster spies have infiltrated government agencies.

A couple of years ago the U.S. Customs Bureau is reported to have received information that an Italian freighter carrying olive oil was scheduled to bring one hundred kilos of heroin into New York. Before the boat landed, customs men, Federal Bureau of Narcotics men and New York City detectives crowded into a warehouse close by the dock and trained their field glasses so they could watch everything that happened when the freighter docked. Their presence in the warehouse was not known to anyone. Yet, when the boat was unloaded and when the olive oil cans were separated according to brand name and destination, everyone shunned the ones that contained the heroin. How could the mob have been tipped off? Only through inside information.

The Italian freighter was not the only boat whose smugglers could not be caught. Everybody in the know believes that the *Ile De France* was a large heroin carrier. The Customs Bureau searched her from stem to stern every time she docked. They never found anything.

Here, then, is the picture. International control has not stopped the mobsters and neither has the Customs Bureau. What about control within our own borders? The Federal Bureau of Narcotics, which, like the Customs Bureau, functions under the Treasury Department, is the main arm for curbing the traffic within this country. For many years the Federal Bureau of Narcotics was handicapped in its work by a staff too small to begin to cope with its monumental responsibilities. In 1952, however, Congress appropriated sufficient money to permit Commissioner Anslinger to increase his staff of agents to the number he considers adequate. The Federal Bureau has put up a vigorous fight against smugglers. Its agents have an overwhelming job. They must have inexhaustible patience and must be ready to spend weeks and months on the trail of a single offender. They must be good actors since they try to infiltrate the ranks of the mobsters by posing as gangmen themselves. Narcotics men must know the language of the addicts and the sellers, since a wrong phrase, a wrong word can lead the mobsters to penetrate their disguises and identify them as "Feds." They must also be able to recognize every known drug by its appearance or taste. And, of course, it goes without saying that they must be fitted to apprehend addicts whom no one else can recognize for what they are.

"It is the addicts who may lead you to the pushers and so on up the line," says on old-time agent. "If you do not recognize them for what they are immediately, you may be wasting valuable time. We usually look for a yellowish tone in the skin of a white addict and a grayish tone in the skin of the Negro. You can recognize "pipes," opium addicts, by the odor which clings to them. Addicts are bound to be stoolies and you never know where they can take you. I've gotten into some interesting mob setups just by relying on my addict stoolies. I've even been able to help break up a couple of dope rings. This job's full of excitement. You never know today what tomorrow will bring."

Actually, for all the dramatic adventures they have and for all their real accomplishments, Federal Bureau men seldom meet the true big shots. The masterminds of the narcotics rings are surrounded by so many defenses against detection that it is a rare agent who can approach them. And while dope rings are smashed now and again, the chieftains are seldom seized. It is the small fry whom the Bureau agents generally meet and arrest.

Virtually the only first-echelon dealer whom the Bureau has nabbed to date has been Vito Genovese. This is an accomplishment, of course, but practically it cannot mean much so long as all the other top men are walking free. The Bureau itself admits that there is a new dope ring to take the place of every one it smashes and that periodic round-ups, even if conducted on a national scale, while they may serve to weaken the racket, never effect a killing blow. Perhaps the biggest round-up in American history was that staged in 1952 by the Federal Bureau of Narcotics with the cooperation of state and local law-enforcement officials, which netted a total of nearly five hundred suspects. But was the syndicate affected by this round-up? Hardly at all.

And so many states have passed narcotics laws designed to supplement and reinforce the effort of the Federal Government. But state enforcement has proved as ineffectual as federal enforcement. Therefore in a number of communities —mainly large cities where the traffic is especially heavy— there are special narcotics squads within local police departments. However, the ability of many narcotics sellers to tempt police officers with large bribes poses a special problem to law enforcement in this area. A recent Congressional inquiry into crime in the nation's capital, together with investigations in other areas, indicated sensational police–drug dealer tie-ups. In some areas, policemen appeared to be on the regular payroll of drug dealers. But even without this difficulty, local agencies cannot ever hurt the syndicate. And it does not matter how bright and dedicated their officers are. Because of the nature of the problem, the effect of local agencies must be, at best, limited.

Perhaps one of the most effective of the local police

departments is that in New York City. Take Eddie Fitz-gerald, one of its outstanding members, as an example of the kind of job its personnel does. Eddie is thirty-two years old. He is a slender, good-looking young man with dark, curly hair and a charming smile. He has been on the force for six years and he has come to be somewhat of a legend in his department.

"You want to know about Eddie?" says his friend and co-worker, big, red-faced, hearty Sol Green. "He's a psy-choanalyst deep down so that anybody who has a story to tell tells it to him. What an actor! He can see a man once and then *be* him. Everybody likes Eddie. He's a smooth talker. He's full of bright ideas. And he's not afraid of any-thing or anyone."

Sol was Eddie's partner during his first assignment in the Squad. A narcotics addict in the New York City Tombs had informed the police that narcotics was being brought into the institution. He hoped to obtain his freedom in exchange for the communication.

"Of course," Eddie says, "that addict was not telling us anything we had not heard before. Everybody knew there was junk in the Tombs. The newspapers had carried the story time and again. But still Sol and I were assigned to ferret it out. We got into a phoney automobile accident and were picked up with a couple of marijuana cigarettes on us. The judge gave up thirty days in the Tombs. We were placed in a cell on the narcotics users' tier. Believe me, going into prison as a stoolie is a gloomy assignment. I saw what the convicts did to one stoolie."

The stoolie, a sickly, weak-faced, elderly man named Sisco, had committed the "unforgiveable crime" of squeal-ing to a neurotic guard about another prisoner who had stolen a ball-bearing pencil to which the guard was pecul-iarly attached. It did not take long before the other con-victs knew what Sisco had done. And almost immediately a muttering began among cells.

"Sisco stooled to the hacks. Let's get Sisco. We got to get Sisco. We'll show him something. We're going to get Sisco."

The next morning, when the guard pressed the button to open the cell doors, about one hundred prisoners crowded around Sisco's cell. They stood body to body in front of the door so that the guard would not know what was going on. While ninety men formed a human wall against the guard, ten picked ones slipped inside Sisco's cell and beat him with their fists. The guards could not hear Sisco scream because the ninety men outside the door talked too loudly. As each man passed Sisco's cell he entered and kicked him. That was so that nobody could be blamed in case he died. After all, if you have one hundred participants in a murder, it is difficult to convict any one of them. The last prisoner to enter Sisco's cell propped him up in his cot and covered him with a blanket.

Sisco lay unconscious from shortly after eight o'clock to eleven. When the guard came through and made a systematic head check he asked Sisco's cellmate, Angelo, "what's the matter with Sisco?"

"He's sick."

"You think he needs a doctor?"

"He told me no. He says he just wants to rest."

The guard took the cellmate's word for Sisco's condition. At three o'clock, however, when he came through for another head check, he lifted the blanket and found Sisco dead. When the prisoners were questioned, nobody knew anything. In jail, nobody ever knows anything about such matters. Sisco's family was told he had died of congestion of the viscera.

"After Sisco died, I was haunted by him," Eddie says. "But what happened to him didn't stop Sol and me from doing our job. Our job was to buy the narcotics if possible and to find how it was getting into prison, and who was controlling it from the outside.

"During the six days we were in the Tombs, we had contact with three separate people, one of whom was the big controller, Tootsie Johnson, and two others who were bringing in barbiturates.

"Yes, they had horse in there. It was the highest grade heroin I had ever seen. It was eighty-three per cent pure. It was coming in at about a quarter of an ounce at a time.

"These were inmates who were getting the heroin into the prison and here's how they worked. In our tier, you are allowed one package of clean clothes a week. Tootsie

Johnson, this big controller, had three very close friends in the place who had no outside contacts to bring them clothes. So what he would do was make contacts to have clothes for them brought to him. His girl would bring clean clothes for them. She would bring a package for Tootsie on Monday, another package for his friend on Wednesday and one for the second friend on Friday. That is three packages of clothes delivered, which is three quarters of an ounce of heroin. These packages would be listed for these other parties but when the guard would bring them in, Tootsie would just get ahold of them, take them up to his cell, remove the narcotics and give the guys the clean clothes. And, like I said, he would get the three quarters of an ounce of stuff practically pure.

"You see, this was a quarter of an ounce of stuff undiluted. Where a narcotics addict is used to taking about three per cent stuff—this is eighty-three per cent stuff—he would need a thumbnail of three per cent stuff to take off. With this he would need maybe an ash speck to take off. Actually when the stuff was laid out it took care of twenty-two or twenty-three people and they were loaded.

"This had been going on apparently for about a year and it was going on when I was in. Tootsie had been in the Tombs for eleven months.

"Well, this particular day, Sol and I had been in about five days and we had reached the point where we were in like crazy. We were into about four separate groups, tight. We had contracted for stuff and given up our soft money. Of course we'd had to smuggle soft money in. It was done by my lawyer's sticking dollar bills onto a wad of gum and the gum onto his hand and shaking hands with me. So, when we shook hands the money was transferred from his hand to mine.

"This night I'm talking about, everything was hunky-dory. The contact was set, the stuff was supposed to be in so we could make our buys. And then all hell broke loose."

It seems that Juan, the informant, had been expecting to get out of jail a couple of days after he had sent out his tip, and here it was, a whole week afterward, and he was still in jail. He felt that the police had let him down, so he told the other inmates about Eddie and Sol.

"Hey, there are two coppers in this jail. They're here to bust the racket."

Juan's message followed a chain from one cell to another. It missed only one cell out of a couple of hundred, the one in which Sol and Eddie were lodged. And while the kite flew, everyone talked to one another:

"Hey, babe?"

"Yeah, man?"

"Thanks for that strawberry shortcake."

"Anytime, baby."

"All right."

"Yeah."

"See you later, man."

The men chuckled, cursed, shook off their lonely feelings by making small passes at one another.

"Hey baby, I thought you were going to sleep in my cell tonight. 'Cause I love you."

"Oh, later for you, man. Tomorrow."

"All right. Don't forget you promised."

Then they began passing small articles to one another.

"Man, give this O'Henry to Pasquale."

"All right."

They went on talking. In jail, talking's one way to keep from breaking down.

"Hey, Patsy?"

"Who is that?"

"This is Jimmy."

"Yeah, what do you want?"

"Hey, Patsy, do you know a broad up on 114th Street?

"Nah. I only know downtown chicks."

After a while the quips and jokes began, the old question-and-answer period.

"Hey man, tell us how you got caught."

"Got caught 'cause this broad said I raped her."

"Oh, a sex clown. Hey, sex. Hey sex, tell us, was it worth it? It has to be 'cause you're going to do ten years. It ought to be good."

On this night, there was a whispering, a hissing under the ordinary conversation. Even the guard felt something in the air. He went from one tier to another, trying to keep an eye on all the men. Once in a while, for no good reason, he yelled out: "Shut up, you."

The men went on talking.

"Who knows what we're going to eat tonight?"

"Beans."

"Oh, no."

"Who said, oh no?"

"Bobby."

"Bobby said oh no?"

"I hate beans."

"What do you mean, you hate beans? All I could hear from you yesterday was shuck, shuck. You sure were shucking those beans down."

After a while, the men's suppers were brought into their cells and the only noise was the sound of their eating. The guards came around to collect the empty trays. Everyone smoked. Everyone, except Eddie and Sol, relaxed. Eddie got his tin cup and polished it on his blanket until he achieved a mirror surface. He held the polished cup up so that he could see what was going on around him. The kites were still flying all over the place. It seemed as though Eddie and Sol were the only ones who did not get notes.

Eddie decided to test the men's hostility. Did anyone feel friendly to Sol and himself? He tapped to the man in the cell next to his.

"Hey, babe?"

"Yeah."

"Let me see your book, man."

"I got no book for you."

"You got the papers?"

"No, I threw them away."

Eddie tried to converse with the man on his other side.

"Have you got a book?"

"I'm sleeping."

"But have you got a book?"

"No, Cap, I got no book."

"How about the paper?"

"I got no paper for you."

Now Eddie was really panicky.

"Well," he asked Sol, "what the hell are we going to do?"

Sol said, "We got to head for the out. Remember what the captain said."

Eddie felt a little relief when he thought of what the captain had told Sol and him before they went into the Tombs.

"Now, anything happens in there and you men are in the least danger, if you men are in the *least* danger you will send a message out. You will phone this code number and you will say that you want your lawyer. It does not matter what hour of the day or night, you say you want your lawyer and you will be released. Look here, men, someone on the Narcotic Squad will be on duty for you twenty-four hours a day. As soon as they receive your call, they will immediately contact the Police Commissioner who will call the Commissioner of Correction who will call· the warden and, believe me, you will be released pronto."

The code number happened to be Eddie's own telephone. His wife was on duty to receive the call. Eddie knew Mona would never leave the phone. He called the guard and gave him fifty cents and the telephone number. He said, "Please call this number immediately." The time was five-thirty.

Then it was six o'clock. Why weren't Eddie and Sol released? Where was the guard, anyhow? At six-thirty the guard walked through Eddie's tier again and Eddie said:

"That call I asked you to make. Anything happen on it?"

"It went out."

"Where's the change?"

"What change?"

"I gave you half a buck."

"Oh, here's the change."

"Did you get an answer on the call?"

"It went out, I told you."

"Well, I will send another one."

The second message was less deadpan than the first. "Please, I called you before, send me the lawyer right away, now, today, immediately."

7:00, 7:15, 8:00, 8:30. Eddie called for the guard again. He walked up grinning.

"Did it go?"

"It went. What do you want from me? You are annoying me. Shut up."

So, Eddie asked him to make another call. This time he made his message more urgent. He also began worrying about Mona. He knew she would never have left the telephone voluntarily.

It was midnight. Eight hours was all that stood between death and the detectives. The cell gates opened at 8:15 in the morning. And then two hundred maddened inmates would come after them.

Now, the men began to taunt the detectives.

"Hey, whatsa matter Eddie, you can't get no telephone message out? It's a shame."

"Rest your body, Sol. Cool. Take it easy, man."

"So look," Sol finally told Eddie, "we got no choice. I'm going to blow the whole thing."

The guard came over when Sol called him. "For Christ's sake, what do you want now? What the hell's going on?"

Sol said, "I am Detective Solomon Green of the Narcotic Squad. This is Detective Edward Fitzgerald. We are here on an undercover assignment. You are to communicate forthwith with the Police Commissioner and tell him we want release immediately."

The guard turned white. He had never made any of the phone calls. He had merely pocketed the money for them. Eddie and Sol were released less than forty-five minutes after they told the guard who they were.

"Well," Eddie asks today, "what do you think came out of Sol's and my experience? Old Tootsie was caught red-handed. We tried to get from him who his connection on the outside was, but he wouldn't talk. Sometimes I wonder why we had to risk our lives. We know that, up until today, junk's still coming into the Tombs."

Chapter 2 How Do You Expect Me to Make a Buy?

Eddie Fitzgerald's most recent assignment concerned a big peddler, "Ears" Sanducci, a heavy-faced man with thick lips and the pointed ears from which he had derived his nickname. Eddie was introduced to Ears by an informant named Mary Magrone. Her husband was in jail and she was working with the Narcotic Squad to ease his time.

On the night Eddie first met Ears, Mary was sitting at his table at Braemar's Bar, a gaudy joint on 124th Street. She seemed to be very drunk when Eddie, dressed in a loud checked suit and an open-neck sport shirt, swaggered in.

"What you doing here?" he asked in a proprietary tone.

Mary acted afraid of him. "I'm having a drink."

"Well, finish your drink and get your rooster out of here."

"I got no bread for a cab."

"Here." He threw a ten-dollar bill on the table.

"I need more than that."

He threw her a twenty.

"It's lonesome home. I got nobody to talk to."

"I'll come see you later."

"Sure?"

"Sure."

Ears, who had been friendly with Mary's husband Joe,

naturally wondered about the relationship between Mary and Eddie. He asked Mary who Eddie was. Eddie answered the question himself.

"My name's Angie and I used to work for Mary's old man." He turned to Mary. "I told you to get out of here. Now why're you still hanging around?"

After Mary had left, Ears questioned Eddie more closely. "So your name's Angie and you worked for Joe. What's with you and his wife then?"

Eddie said, "Nothing. Her old man's dropped and I don't want her around in public places. How do I know the coppers ain't trailing her? Have a drink on me and forget it."

"Well, how come you worry so much about her?"

"Her guy and me were tight when he was on the outs. That's how come."

Eddie spent a long time cultivating Ears. He hung around Braemar's with him night after night, buying him drinks and dinners. He learned Ears' weaknesses and strengths. He discovered that Ears' vanity was even greater than that of most of those in the racket and he constantly catered to it. He behaved as though Ears was a wise and knowing man and he always asked him for advice. No wonder Ears liked being with Eddie and began, gradually, to consider him a friend. After about four months, he offered to sell him narcotics.

"Of course, I was very happy about my contact with Ears," Eddie says. "He was a big guy. But I was scared, too. You see, when you start moving in Ears' league, you've got to pretend to be a big buyer. I mean, you've got to be able to make a fifteen-hundred, two-thousand-dollar buy. Well, where can I get that kind of money? Certainly not from my department. I'll never forget what happened between me and the inspector when I told him I had finally gotten Ears lined up."

The inspector was very pleased. He congratulated Eddie.

"Sir," Eddie asked, "may I have fifteen hundred dollars for making my buy with?"

The inspector laughed. "Are you kidding? Fifteen hundred dollars?"

"Well, how much can I get?"

"A hundred and a half."

"Jeez, Inspector, *you* must be kidding. What can I do

with a hundred and a half? I'm not going for Camels or Chesterfields. This is horse. And Ears is tough. He'd blow my brains out."

"We got no money."

"Listen, Ears is used to selling five, six ounces at a time. He wouldn't bother with me."

"We got no money."

"All right, what's the most I can get?"

"Three hundred."

What could Eddie hope to accomplish with three hundred dollars? He knew too well that Ears was accustomed to dealing with men who bought ten, twenty, thirty thousand dollars' worth of drugs at a time. Certainly he would get suspicious of Eddie and his three hundred dollars. There was no telling what his suspicion might drive him to. And still, because he was a policeman and because policemen are disciplined to take orders, Eddie felt he had no choice but to do as the inspector said. When an inspector talks, a policeman listens. So Eddie took his three hundred dollars and went back uptown to find Ears. He located him in Braemar's.

"Listen, Ears, I like to start copping with you."

"O.K. How much you want?"

"Just by a freak, Ears, I only want to pick up a ounce tonight."

"You crazy? The best stuff in the country. I don't bother with no ounces."

Eddie said, "I tell you, Ears, I can't afford to go whole hog because I got too much money tied up in some sympathetic stuff."

"What do you mean, sympathetic?"

"You know, sympathetic—phoney." Eddie knew that Ears would feel more kindly to him if he could correct his English.

Ears smiled. "Oh, you mean synthetic. It's *synthetic,* not sympathetic."

"That's right, Ears, synthetic."

"Well," Ears said, pleased because he had been able to teach Eddie something, "I'll sell you your one ounce this time. But no more." He sent Roberto, one of his runners, to the plant where his drugs were supposed to be stored. Two Squad men followed Roberto. But when Roberto had left and they searched the apartment he had gone into, they could not find more than a few ounces of narcotics. Obviously this was not Ears' main plant. When they called the sergeant who was in charge of their team, he said, "Don't do anything more about the plant and tell Eddie to come see me."

The sergeant told Eddie that he would have to make a big buy so that Ears would lead the detectives to his main plant. He then went with him to the inspector's office. The inspector gave Eddie four thousand dollars.

"Here," he said, "is four thousand dollars. You are responsible for every nickel of this money. You are not to let it out of your hands."

"I am not to let it out of my hands? How do you expect me to make a buy if I am not to let the money out of my hands?"

"Buddy, that's up to you."

"Inspector," Eddie said, "suppose he won't give me the stuff until I give him the money?"

"You are never to let the money out of your hands."

"Well, if he insists on having it, what'll I do, blow the case?"

"You are to get the commodity and make the arrest."

Eddie wished he could tell the inspector what he was thinking—that's a lot easier to say than to do. He was afraid of Ears, desperately afraid. Yet the thrill of the chase was in him, too. More than that, he knew that if he cracked the main plant of Ears Sanducci, he would be eligible for promotion. If he cracked it and stayed alive, it would be an accomplishment of which to be proud. But he had not been fooling when he had told the inspector "Ears can blow my brains out." Well, the inspector was taking a calculated risk with him, Eddie, as the pawn. He would risk an officer's life before he would spend four thousand dollars of the Department's money. It was sickening. But a job's a job. Eddie went back to Braemar's and sat down at Ears' table.

"Now I can talk business, Ears. I want to buy some big stuff. How much of a break will you give me if I say thirty pieces?"

"My stuff's going for two hundred a ounce. But, for you, I'll lean. I'll knock it down to a hundred fifty."

"Make it a hundred and a quarter."

"How much you going to need from now on?"

"The same every week. Thirty pieces."

"O.K. I'll lean. A hundred and a quarter for you. When'll you have the vigorish?"

"Give me a day or so."

"Solid."

Eddie was to meet Ears on 116th Street and Second Avenue at twelve o'clock the next night. He was there on time and so were his tails. His two bosses, the sergeant and the captain, sat in a tan De Soto across the street from where he waited and Sol Green and another detective walked on the same side. At 12:40, Ears pulled up in a black Chrysler Eddie had never seen before and told him to get in. He began driving toward the Bronx. The Bronx? Why was Ears going there? It was threatening territory to Eddie because he and Sol had arrested the fierce Salvatore Santora in the Bronx and Santora had a twenty-five thousand dollar reward out for them. Dead or alive.

"Ears," Eddie asked, pretending a confidence he was far from feeling, "where are we going?"

"The Bronx."

"Where in the Bronx?"

"The Bronx." Ears had never been so short with Eddie before.

They drove to White Plains Road and Bruckner Boulevard, Salvatore Santora's territory. Eddie kept looking in the mirror for his bosses' car. He could not see it. Where were the bosses? And where was Sol? Eddie had come to depend on Sol during his hardest assignments. Somehow, the sight of Sol bolstered him. And, tonight of all nights, Sol wasn't around. Tonight of all nights, Eddie was alone.

Ears parked, took his keys and walked out of the car. He told Eddie, "You stay here 'til I come back."

When Ears came back, he was accompanied by a tall, husky man who looked a lot like Salvatore Santora. Eddie thought to himself, all right, Ears knows I'm a policeman and he's playing cat and mouse with me. He's brought me up here to Salvatore, so he can collect the twenty-five thousand and get rid of me at the same time. What'll I do, sit quietly and take my chances or try to fight? Where are my tails anyhow? Where are my bosses? Where's Sol?

But the man with Ears turned out to be someone named Red Mazzuni. When he climbed into the car, Eddie saw that Red didn't really look like Santora, except in build. Red had a pugilist's face, with a flattened nose and a mop of carroty hair.

Ears said, "Angie, meet my boy, Red. " Eddie forced a smile. "Hi, Red."

Red said, "You got the bread?"

"Sure."

"Give it up."

"What do you mean, give it up."

"Give me the bread."

"I can't do that."

Now, Ears spoke. "Dig, Sonny, Red's my boy. What do you mean you can't give him the bread? If you don't trust him, you don't trust me."

"Well, now look, baby, I trust you. I give you the bread for one ounce, two ounces, but this is thirty-seven fifty."

"Do you think I'm going to jump for thirty-seven fifty? Are you out of your mind? Give me the bread."

"What do you mean, give it? Look, it may not be anything to you 'cause you are a big connection. Cap, it's a lot to me because it's not all mine. You know that."

"What are you worrying about? There is nothing to worry about. Thirty-seven fifty? Are you crazy? What do you think my car is worth? Forty-six hundred? Here, I'll sign my car over to you. What do you mean, thirty-seven fifty and you can't give it up to me? Are you out of your mind?"

"Baby, I would love to do it but I can't do it. Why do you want the money so fast? Let me see the stuff. Like you may switch it and give me some glue. You know?"

"Who's going to give you glue? Do you think we're bums? If you want to do business, give us the money. We don't want to walk with money and junk. Give us the money, and we will bring the junk back."

"Give me the junk first. I want to see it first."

"Why do you want to see it first? It's the same as you got before. What do you want to see it first for?"

Now, Ears was becoming angry. He was yelling at Eddie. And Eddie did not like the way Ears looked at him. He thought from Ears' voice and his looks that the mobster was growing disgusted with him. If he was, he might order Red to shoot things out. Ears had killed for lesser reasons. In a panic, Eddie said, "Look, I'll tell you what, babe. Let me call my people and tell them I've got a little trouble here. Like I know you're a good connection but they would want me to see the stuff. Give me a chance, huh?"

Ears drove Eddie to a restaurant where he could make his call. He accompanied him into the phone booth because he obviously did not trust him to go alone. Eddie dialed the number of the New York Narcotic Squad.

"Narcotic squad, Detective Jones."

"Hey, babe, how you doing man? I'm sorry to be calling you so late."

"What? This is the Narcotic Squad."

"Yeah, babe, I'm wise. This is Angie, you know."

"What? Is that you, Eddie?"

"Yeah, babe."

"What's wrong?"

"I'm having a little trouble with my people here. Like the deal is still on, you know, but they want me to front the bread, catch. . . ."

Detective Jones said, "Unh hunh. What do you want?"

"Tell the people, you know, that I'm on the scene."

"Yeah, they've been calling the last hour. Where are you?"

"I'm at some place in the Bronx like. Solly Boy knows."

Sol knew the Santora territory. "Is Solly Boy still there?"

"Yeah, he's still on 116th Street."

After the call, Ears, Red and Eddie drove back to Bruckner Boulevard. The conversation between Eddie and Ears continued the way it had been going. "You *got* to front the bread, man," and "Man, I *can't* front the bread. My people won't like it, baby, you know."

Finally, Ears made Eddie a proposition: "Angie, I tell you what I'm going to do. I'll give you a break. Red's going to go pick up on the stuff. You and me's going to drive around the corner. The third time we'll meet up with Red, scc? That's when you give me the bread. I get out of the car, Red gets in. He gives you the stuff, you drive another block and you both get out. Okay, babe?"

"Sure, man."

Ears parked the car and Red got out.

"Pass the bread, babe."

"Man, I can't do it. Like, my people. . . ."

"Pass the bread."

The car, with Ears driving, had rounded the corner three times and Ears got out and Red got in. And what finally happened to Eddie Fitzgerald was like something out of a dime novel. Just as Red had said, "I'll kill you if you don't give me the bread," Eddie's tails rode in.

"Whew," Eddie tells, "you can bet I felt better when I saw that De Soto coming. But I was burned at what happened after all my work. Red was caught in possession of thirty ounces, and pleaded guilty. At Ear's trial, Red called me a liar for saying he worked for Ears. 'The copper's a liar,' he said, 'I ain't working for nobody but me, myself and I.' Ears beat the rap. Well, the way I figure it, we aren't going to get the big boys and we can get our brains blown out while we try. Honestly, I sometimes wonder what I'm doing in the Squad."

Chapter 3 Potential Birds

There are many honest Narcotic Squad officers who are discouraged and repelled by the hypocrisy of their jobs. Many detectives wonder, as does Eddie Fitzgerald, why they are risking their lives night after night. "If the big shots are immune," they say, "and the addicts can't be stopped, what is the point of all we are doing?" That is a question that all of us ought to ask ourselves. But we cannot answer it because we are too confused by the inconsistent thinking underlying our present narcotics laws. These laws tell us, for example, that narcotics peddlers must be jailed because they injure addicts. Are our laws then designed to save addicts from peddlers? Of course not, since addicts are sent to prison much more often than are non-addicted peddlers. Actually the laws protect the racketeers, for the frequent arrests of addicts deceive the public into believing that drug profiteers are being dealt with severely, when the truth, as Eddie Fitzgerald points it up, is exactly opposite to what it seems.

"I hate to admit this," Eddy says, "but I think that most coppers get tired of beating their heads against a wall after a while and they start going after the small fry instead of the big men. Truthfully speaking, every cop is out to make a record and impress his superiors. Of course you can do that if you nail a big shot but your chances of getting one are very small. Sometimes you spend months on a case

115

and then it blows up in your face the way that Ears business blew up in mine. And your bosses get mad at you. I won't even mention the fact that you can't get the kind of money you need to make your buys. You want to know if I could hope to catch a big shot? Well, if I had an unlimited expense account and all the time in the world, I might have some chance of doing it. I don't blame my bosses for not staking me to that. But they can't blame me for learning what I have to do after a while. I concentrate on nabbing the little guys. I don't mean just addicts. I mean junkie pushers too. They'll all chirp. All junkies are potential birds. All you have to do is recognize them and say you're going to pull them in and each of them will offer you a dozen names of other pushers, junkies of course. But, what's the difference? It doesn't matter whether they're addicted or not. You make your record on the number of arrests you make and junkies are so easy to get. I'm telling you, all you have to say to someone who needs junk is 'I'm taking you in, bud,' and he'll answer all your questions. He'll do anything."

Eddie Fitzgerald is right when he says an addicted person, whether pusher or plain addict, will do anything to stay out of jail. And there is a reason for his perfidy. Of course, he'll never tell the truth about it. He'll mislead one with talk about the physical aspects of withdrawal, the yawning and the sweating, the vomiting and the diarrhea. He'll moan about the bones that feel broken and the muscles that feel wrenched. And he'll never mention the elements that really terrify him. He won't talk about his fear of losing his mind, about his inability to face the hate and the evil in him. In him as in everybody. But what does he know about other people? He won't talk about the self-contempt he's got to face when he hasn't got drugs, or about the maggoty memories that go unwinding in his head.

All the same, it is those elements, the fear and the self-contempt and the maggoty memories that can turn a man into a mouse or a long-tailed rat. You musn't get busted. You'll die if you're busted. Certainly, he'd stool rather than go to prison and do without his narcotics. He knows he may die anyhow. He knows all about omerta. The big boys are not making allowances for the fact that he's weak and a little sick in the head. They'd still give him a hot shot as soon as look at him. An addict can't help himself, though. He's got to take his chance today. He's not the kind to think about tomorrow. He might not be on stuff if he were.

But what about our law that uses a man's weakness to compel him to act as a stool pigeon and rewards him for the act? After all, the addict who "cooperates" is allowed to continue his habit and is either exempted from punishment or given a lighter sentence. The police use various devices, both direct and indirect to allow the stool to get his drugs. They may give him, for his own use, some of the heroin which he has bought as evidence, or they may locate a doctor who will prescribe for him. Sometimes they give him money and do not ask what he does with it.

These police methods are seldom revealed in court. But one cannot escape the impression that detectives sometimes perjure themselves in order to cover them up. Despite the perjury, however, most judges believe that these unsavory methods are used. They say that they are "filthy," but necessary if the law is to be enforced.

"Of course," says Eddie Fitzgerald, "the junkie special employee [police parlance for stool pigeon] usually helps you put your hands on other addicts, not big peddlers."

And Alfred R. Lindesmith, author of *Opiate Addiction* and Professor of Sociology at Indiana University, remarks ironically, "The 'built-in' third degree is not available to the police when they deal with the big men in the dope traffic who are not addicts."

Professor Lindesmith also points out that an addict's usefulness is not likely to last long, and that when it is over, the police may get rid of him by the practice known as "burning"—revealing him as a stool pigeon to other addicts and peddlers.

Joey Coro served as a Narcotic Squad stoolie until recently. He is twenty-one years old, good-looking and intelligent, but a long-term addict. Although he'd always wanted to be an actor, he works as a grocery clerk. He supplements his income by small-time drug peddling.

"I was caught selling horse to three kids, sixteen and seventeen years old," he tells. "The copper who picked me up said, 'You may not know it, man, but selling to teeners is the big wallop today. You can get the electric chair or

go to the pen for life.' I was scared plenty when I heard
him talk. Besides, I just had had an awful fight with my
wife and I felt like I had to see her again. I was glad to have
the opportunity to stool. Well, not glad. But at least I could
get back to Louisa if I did. I could tell her I was sorry for
everything."

On the night of one of their worst quarrels, which had
become more and more frequent, Joey and Louisa were
still at dinner in the kitchen of their grubby three-room
apartment. As usual, the fight had begun over their son,
Joey, Jr.

"Who wants that kid?" Joey had wailed out. "You know
damn well I never wanted a kid."

He has a spirit of defeatism in him and whenever he
needs a shot he feels he can not secure a decent future
for his son.

Louisa stood and looked at him, tremulous, vulnerable.
"You're sick again."

"Damn right, you lousy son-of-a-bitch." In a state like
this, distorted by his panic, his need for heroin, he gets a
vicious gratification from hitting out at her. One shot, he
thought, one shot and I'll be O.K. "You stinking little
bastard," he shouted at her.

Louisa said, "For God's sake, don't talk to me like that."

"Can the religious crap." He looked at her as though she
were a stranger, his face hard, his eyes cold.

And the quarrel grew more explosive between them. Joey's
talk got wilder. But then, as always, it toned down.

"God, Louisa, you know I don't mean a word of what I
said to you. I don't want to keep hammering at you of all
people."

Louisa has always forgiven him when he told her he was
sorry. But not today.

"I don't know, Joey, sometimes I go to bed and I wonder
what's wrong with me."

"Listen, you're wonderful, much too good. . . ."

"I go to bed and think to myself, any decent woman
couldn't love such a man. It isn't just that I'm afraid of you
when you get the way you did just now. That's terrible
enough, to live with a man and be afraid of him all the

time, but that's not what makes me feel so rotten. It's that I've been even more afraid of losing you than I have of making you angry. A man like you and I've been afraid to lose him. Tell me, Joey, what kind of a woman would worry over losing a man like you?"

"Yeah," Joey said, "you're right, honey. I know how it is. If I was any kind of a man, I'd walk out and never come back again. I'd leave you."

And because she is human and healthy and hungry for his love, because there is a whole lot of woman's warmth in her, Louisa always clung when Joey talked that way before. This time, though, she threw away her woman's warmth.

"Yeah, Joey, if you were a man, you would walk out."

"Your mother'd be thrilled if I left. Your father too."

"Anybody's parents would be thrilled. Mine'd think I'd got my pride back. Every time I see Mama, she asks me where it's gone to, my pride, I mean." Louisa began to cry, but on her own account for a change, not Joey's.

Joey grew frightened. He said "I'm going to ask you a question and you got to answer it honestly. God, Louisa, do you *want* me to walk out?"

She whimpered something he couldn't understand.

"You got to tell me. Otherwise, how'm I going to know? I'm not talking about your family now. I don't care what they want. You're the only one I care for. Listen, Louisa, there's only one thing could make me go away from you. If you tell me to."

"Joey."

"What, sweetheart?"

"I want you to go. Now, tonight, before I change my mind."

"I love you."

"You asked me and I told you."

And then she looked up, saw his remorseful eyes and his poor anguished face and she had to open her heart up to him. She kissed him, and her lips clung to his in passionate pity. She threw her arms around his neck and held him to her. Then, almost wantonly, she began pulling him toward the bed. He wanted to go with her—for her sake if not his own—and yet he could not stop to make love to her then. He had to get his shot. The sickness was coming on. His hands and feet were growing numb. The light was bothering his eyes. He was beginning to perspire.

"I'll be back soon. I promise, sweetheart. Don't go to bed 'til I come."

She was breathing heavily—with passion, indignation. "Why?"

"Why what, honey baby?"

"Why shouldn't I go to bed 'til you come back?"

He couldn't bring himself to lie to her. She knew how long it had been since he'd really wanted her. Besides, his affliction was driving him harder. He couldn't just stand around talking. "Look, I got to go, Louisa."

"And I got to have what other women do. I'm human, Joey Coro. You haven't touched me in.... Listen, if you want me here when you come back, you'll remember that I count for something, too. You won't let me stand here pleading with you, lowering myself like, like I was a piece of garbage or something. You'll.... Oh, Joey, you know what you'll do."

He stood and looked at her, torn between her need and his own. And because he was stunned by her expression, because he was made miserable by the guilt he felt toward her, he saw her for a moment as a stupid woman, greedy for her satisfaction while he was in anguish. He began to beat her. He struck her blindly, again and again.

And now, here he was, sick and fuzzy-eyed, picked up for selling to teen-agers. And the narcotics detective was threatening him. "You can get the electric chair. You can go to jail for life."

Then the detective offered Joey an opportunity to save himself.

"You know junkies?"

"Yes, sir."

"Pushers?"

"Yes, sir."

"You want to cooperate with us, kid? You want to work with us?"

"Yes, sir."

"All right, tomorrow, we'll introduce you to one of our

women detectives. Her name's Margo Dryer. You'll take her around and introduce her to people."

"Yes, sir."

And that is the story of why Joey Coro came to be walking with Margo Dryer down Fred C. Delvi's and Joe Babes,' and Mimi Marano's and his own home base.

"Joey," Margo asked, "got your story straight?"

"I guess."

Margo said, "I don't want to sound like a schoolteacher, but I'd like you to repeat it a couple of times before Fatsy comes."

Fatsy was the connection from whom Joey bought his narcotics.

Joey said, "I tell Fatsy you're a downtown chick. I know you're O.K. You used to be in a house but now you've got a couple of your own girls on the string. You buy stuff for all of them. You buy big. You used to have a fine connection but he got busted. That's how come I brought you to Fatsy."

Margo smiled. 'How soon do you think the bum'll show?" she asked. Her fragile, golden prettiness was difficult to reconcile with her whiskey voice and gawky words.

Before Joey could answer, a woman came by and thrust close to him. He felt that his secret passed from him to her. Joey Coro, banana for the coppers. He needed his shot. He said, "I got to go home for a minute."

"O.K., Joey, go on. I'll wait here for you."

Margo knew Joey was going for his heroin, but she did not try to stop him.

Joey got to his house, walked into the bedroom and fingered the works gently. He tightened the band around his arm. He stuck the needle into his arm and he relaxed, anticipating the relief. Now, the heroin flooded his being. His shivering stopped. The haze was gone from his eyes. And, most important, he felt that now he could talk to Margo Dryer or anyone. When he went out on the street again and found Margo, he said:

"I guess we better hurry up to Rollo's. Fatsy always shows around now."

Joey and Margo stood outside of Rollo's waiting for Fatsy and watching everyone who walked by. Margo acted like the prostitute she was portraying for the night. Men regarded her with that look they reserve for prostitutes and near-prostitutes. It was as though they would stroke her with their fingers. One man asked her:

"Hey, how's about it, sister?"

"Not tonight, Josephine," she said.

What an act she puts on, Joey thought. Watching Margo, he was filled with resentment toward his father, who had laughed the idea of acting out of his head. Whenever he is high on heroin, he feels he could have been an actor, if his father had only encouraged him. This night, he thought, Margo's not the only one who can act. I can too. I'm as good as anybody.

And, when big, lumbering Fatsy finally arrived at Rollo's and he and Joey and Margo took a table, Joey was able to put on the act the Squad had asked him to.

"Dig, Fatsy, like this is Joan Merrill. Joanie, Fatsy." He patted himself on the back because before he had taken this last shot, he had feared that he would forget the name Joan Merrill and get into more trouble by calling her Margo Dryer. He said, "Fatsy, Joanie's a working chick. She's got a stable of junkies. She cops for them. But her connection got busted."

Fatsy laughed. "Since when *you* going with working chicks, Joey? And junkies besides."

Margo, evidently not trusting Joey, began talking to Fatsy herself.

"I'm not on the stuff, myself, Fatsy, but I cop for my old lady as well as those girls I got working for me."

"How many work for you?"

"Three."

"All on junk, you say?"

"Yup."

"What about your old lady? What's her habit?"

"Forty a day. And she needs it bad. She'd die if she couldn't get it."

"I'm sorry for your old lady, Joan, but I don't know what Joey brought you here for. I couldn't help you, you know, I don't know anybody who deals in the junk. I'm in the plumbing and heating business myself. Joey, what'd you tell this chick about me?"

Margo smiled. "Just that you're a good friend of his."

Fatsy said, "Joey, I still want to know what you're doing with working chicks."

Joey, still the superb actor in his mind, thought fast. "You see," he said, "Joanie's my cousin."

He was flattered at the effect his story had on Fatsy. For the first time, the fat man seemed to believe what he was being told. "Like, dig that," he said, "who could tell this chick's a wop?"

Joey's job was finished. Now Margo must be left alone to cultivate Fatsy and to soften him up if she could. Joey left feeling triumphant.

"I thought I'd put on a great act," he says today. "You always think you're fine with horse in you. I carried on a silent conversation with my father. I told him, 'You said I couldn't act, Pa, didn't you? You should have seen me tonight. I was great. You'd have had to say so yourself.' But, half an hour later, I no longer felt so smart. The horse had worn off and I kept thinking, 'I broke omerta. I—broke—omerta. What's going to happen to me now?' "

BOOK IV

**Deliver
Our
Children**

Chapter **1 Death Sentence**

What happens to the Joey Coros, the frightened, small-time pushers who tell the police what they know, although they don't know too much? Joey didn't tell about the Genoveses, the Barbettas, the Fred C. Delvis. He didn't talk about any right men, any big men. How could he have? He does not know their names. He only exposed a small-timer out of his own world. Still, he broke omerta and it's likely he will die for doing it. Everyone knows that there have been numbers of Joeys mysteriously slain in recent years.

Still, some of those in authority defend the use of stool pigeon addicts like Joey Coro on the ground that they are habitual criminals and deserve whatever happens to them. At the same time, they say they recognize that addicts are sick. Is it fair then to be so indifferent to the safety and welfare of sick people? And what about the fact that when enforcement agencies use stoolies they inevitably become involved in violations of the very laws they claim to be enforcing?

Despite their own transgressions, and expressedly decent sentiments toward addicts, the enforcement agencies vigorously demand ever harsher penalties and ever stiffer laws against addiction. What can they hope to accomplish with their stiffer laws? After all, the punitive, prohibitory approach to the drug problem has been the official policy

127

of the United States for forty years. No other country in the world has been so sadistic in dealing with addicts. Still there are more addicts in the United States today than in all the other Western countries combined, and more juvenile users in New York City than in all Europe.

Surely the situation requires that we reflect on our experience, and consider a change in attitude. Maybe our present policy is ill conceived. Instead of reconsidering our policy, however, we have continued to build upon it over the years.

The punitive approach to addiction traces back to 1914, when the United States Congress passed a statute known as the Harrison Act. Essentially, the Harrison Act is neither a criminal statute nor a prohibition act but rather a revenue act designed to regulate the drug traffic. It requires everyone through whose hands drugs pass—importers, manufacturers, wholesalers, retailers and doctors to register and pay a tax. They have to use a special order form for legal transfer so that the government can check on the origin and ultimate use of all drugs. Actually the government, in 1914, sought no interference with legitimate medical practice or medical treatment of addicts, since the Harrison Act specifically provides that the act "shall not apply to the dispensing, or administration, or giving away of narcotic drugs to a patient by a registered physician, . . . in the course of his professional practice, and where said drugs are dispensed or administered to the patient for legitimate medical purposes, . . ."

The Harrison Act went largely unnoticed for some five years after its enactment in 1914. But in 1919 a special Treasury Department committee aroused the nation with an absurd report that one million persons in the United States had become addicted to drugs. Other reports followed with estimates that ran as high as five million. Then, curiously at the instance of leaders of the medical profession itself, the Treasury Department launched an all-out attack on doctors administering drugs to addicts in the course of therapy.

In 1919, a doctor, John Webb, was accused of selling drug prescriptions. Dr. Webb had been guilty of flagrant abuse. He had been selling prescriptions by the thousands, indiscriminately to any person, for fifty cents apiece. He was of course found guilty. He appealed his conviction all the way to the Supreme Court. The Government asked for an authoritative expression as to what constituted the legitimate practice of medicine in dealing with addicts. The question certified to the Supreme Court was this:

"If a practicing and registered physician issues an order for morphine to an habitual user thereof, the order not being issued by him in the course of professional treatment in the attempted cure of the habit, but being issued for the purpose of providing the user with morphine sufficient to keep him comfortable by maintaining his customary use, is such order a physician's prescription under exception (b) of section 2 [of the Harrison Act]?"

The question was wholly unrelated to the facts of the case. But, influenced by the public hysteria that had been so effectively created, and the obvious guilt of the defendant, the Supreme Court (5–4) answered the question as follows:

"To call such an order for the use of morphine a physician's prescription would be so plain a perversion of meaning that no discussion is required."

The Webb case was soon followed by several other cases which reached the Supreme Court. These cases, like the Webb case, were presented by the government in a manner cunningly designed to get the desired ruling, and the decisions, like the Webb decision, did tend to support the position of the Treasury Department. A reign of terror then ensued. The Narcotics Bureau proceeded to warn doctors against prescribing drugs for the purpose of avoiding withdrawal distress or keeping addicts comfortable. Most doctors became intimidated and stopped treating addicts altogether. The few who had the effrontery to persist in caring for them were prosecuted and imprisoned. One doctor, however, appealed his conviction successfully. His case, *Linder v. United States,* reached the Supreme Court in 1925. By this time public hysteria had subsided; the Court reversed itself and completely vindicated Dr. Charles O. Linder. A unanimous opinion set forth an interpretation of the Harrison Act which is to this day the law of the land:

It [the Harrison Act] says nothing of addicts and does not undertake to prescribe methods of their medical treatment. They are
diseased and proper subjects for medical treatment, and we cannot possibly conclude that a physician acted improperly or un-
wisely or for other than medical purpose solely because he has
dispensed to one of them, in the ordinary course and in good
faith, four small tablets of morphine or cocaine for relief of conditions incident to addiction.

The Court also warned that its opinions in the previous
cases should be narrowly limited to the facts there involved.

Nonetheless, the Treasury Department had accomplished
its purpose. It proceeded to ignore the opinion of the
Supreme Court in the Linder case, and to this day continues to ignore it. In the words of Rufus King, a leader
in the American Bar Association and an authority on narcotics
enforcement: "By 1925, it was too late to change the pattern.
The trick had worked. The doctors had withdrawn, and
they never permitted the addict to re-approach them. The
peddler had taken over, and his profits soared as enforcement
efforts reduced his competition and drove his customers
ever deeper into the underworld, where they were easy prey."

Save for the rare doctor who virtually abandons his
profession and exploits his license to become a veritable
dope pusher, there are no doctors willing to treat addicts
and thus be forced to litigate the matter with the Treasury
Department. Lawyers may indeed counsel the medical profession that the law of the land is that expressed by the
Supreme Court of the United States in *Linder v. United
States*. But an individual doctor can hardly be expected to
challenge the Treasury Department in reliance on such
opinions. He would place in jeopardy his license to practice
medicine. He would expose himself to the risk of temporary
detention or even prolonged incarceration. And even though
ultimately successful, he would meanwhile have incurred
the cost and experienced the harassment, humiliation and
embarrassment inherent in criminal litigation. And so, despite
the pronouncements of the Supreme Court, the law of the
land tends to be obscured by bureaucratic policy that is
contrary to law, and the medical practitioner is effectively
prevented from caring for addicts.

Not only have the doctors fallen for what Rufus King

calls the Treasury Department "trick," but public opinion supports the Department and is hostile to the addict. Accordingly, in 1951, Congress enacted the Boggs Law which increased the already severe mandatory penalties against narcotics violators. Many people said, at the time the law was passed, that it was unjust because its penalties fall mainly upon the victims of the traffic—the addicts—rather than upon the dope racketeers. Indeed, Assistant Attorney General Warren Olney, III, who was at the time in charge of the Criminal Division of the United States Department of Justice, told the Boggs subcommittee:

"Probably the most serious difficulty with the narcotics laws is the fact that they make no distinction between the violator who is a profiteering racketeer and the violator who, in many respects, is a victim of the drug itself, the addict. The same law is applicable to both and they are also subject to the same penalties. Unfortunately the addict and the petty pusher are much more easily apprehended than the major trafficker, who is the source of supply and is several echelons removed from the last seller who deals with the illicit consumer. The result is that the present severe penalties are more often applied to the relatively minor violator than to the big shot against whom they were designed."

Still, in 1956, the Eighty-fourth Congress passed additional unimaginably cruel legislation. By its terms a forty-year sentence with no provision for parole can be imposed on a third conviction for a narcotics offense, and if the conviction is for a sale made to a person eighteen years or under, a death sentence may be given for a *first* offense.

In addition, a number of states have followed the lead of the federal government and enacted statutes that are referred to as "little Boggs Acts."

In California, unlawful possession of narcotics, formerly punishable by the maximum of six years in the state prison, has been increased to a maximum of ten years. Twenty years may be given for a second offense. Ohio, which formerly gave a maximum of five years imprisonment for illegal possession of drugs, now has a maximum sentence of fifteen years for a first offense; a second offense can draw twenty years and a third offense, thirty. In Illinois, illegal possession formerly brought a maximum of one year in the county jail. It is now punishable by two to ten years in the penitentiary for a first offense and by five years to life for subsequent offenses. In Michigan, unlawful possession, formerly punishable by a maximum of four years imprisonment, can now bring a maximum of ten years for a first offense, twenty years for a second offense and twenty to forty years for a third offense.

Can it be that the Congress honestly believed that the new penalties would affect the large mobsters at whom they are supposed to be aimed? R. Tieken, United States Attorney in Chicago, testified as follows at a Congressional hearing to consider the 1956 bill:

The narcotics importer and wholesaler are professionals. They have plenty of money, powerful allies and expert knowledge of how to evade the law and escape detection. They are not addicts and seldom handle drugs, themselves. They have no bank accounts and deal only in cash. Their errands are run by others who transport the drugs and conduct the sales.

To convict the big operator is a difficult task and we fully appreciate that we are nowhere near the big operator when we arrest the pusher who sells to the addict. Even when the pusher tells all he knows, we only reach the dealer—merely one step up the ladder. The ladder may have several steps before it reaches the big importer and the profits from distributing and importing narcotics are enormous.

There was only one measure suggested for getting at the big shots and this, a clause providing for legalized wiretapping, was deleted before the bill was passed.

But even suppose that a big shot were to be convicted, how would he be affected by the 1956 law? According to Professor Lindesmith, "It is a further absurdity that the new narcotics laws do not necessarily increase the penalties against the large operators." In 1936, he says, fifteen years before the Boggs Act, the Federal Bureau of Narcotics broke up a dope ring which had operated in Texas, obtaining its supplies from a source in Chicago which in turn had gotten them from a higher source in New York. The six principals were convicted and received punishment as follows: L. Ginsberg, fifty years and a $10,000 fine; E. D. Salay, G. Payne and J. C. Allen, twenty years and a $2000 fine each; J. Walker, seventeen years and $3000; U. Eichenbaum, ten years and $2000.

Although these men were not big shots but rather fairly important middle-echelon dealers, offenders of their caliber are not very often caught, and are therefore usually first offenders. Were they tried today, under the 1956 law, the maximum mandatory penalties applicable to them would be ten years.

The situation would be laughable if it were not so tragic. For, as the Eighty-fourth Congress ought to have known, the Joey Coros, the sick, driven addicts, are the only ones who are ever arrested as repeated offenders. They are the only ones who sell to teen-agers. They can't help themselves. How else are they going to raise the money they need to keep them functioning? The high cost of illicit drugs drives them to do what they do. And the police have always taken credit for high black market prices, calling them an index of their efficiency. They also say that high prices discourage addiction. This argument is easily disproved, of course, when one considers the dimensions of our present-day drug problem.

It is an absurd and ineffective law that provides life imprisonment for sick addicts and permits the murder merchants to keep going on their way.

Of course, nobody can blame those in authority because the big mobsters are beyond them. But they are to be blamed for pretending that stiffer penalties are intended to get at the big shots, when, as a practical matter, they are directed at the Joey Coros and nobody else.

Why do we keep hounding the Joey Coros? What sense does it make to throw them in jail or to kill them off? We ought to know by now that no matter how harshly we treat addicts, until there is a fundamental change in federal policy, addiction in this country will not be stamped out because the underworld moguls do not intend to get out of so profitable a business. And, when their old customers are jailed, they have ways and means of creating new ones. There are potential victims all around. In a way, the big shots of the narcotics trade must be grateful for the government's single-minded attitude toward addiction.

Just as rumrunning made the Mafia rich when liquor was outlawed in this country, so junkrunning makes the new Mafia rich and powerful today. Our drug laws are immoral in principle and ineffectual in operation.

Chapter **2 Compulsion and Cure**

And yet our Eighty-fourth Congress, the same Eighty-fourth Congress which spawned the Boggs Act decreeing that Joey Coro could be given the death penalty, selfrighteously stated that we ought to undertake to cure addicts as well as to punish them. Cure, gentlemen? What cure? How is cure possible so long as the Treasury Department receives official sanction for persisting in its present vicious policy? How is cure possible so long as we continue to build jails instead of hospitals?

The two federal hospitals in the country, the one in Lexington, Kentucky, and the one in Fort Worth, Texas, have a combined capacity of less than twenty-five hundred. Riverside Hospital in New York City, the only other narcotics hospital in the country, has a capacity of approximately one hundred eighty and is exclusively for addicts under twenty-one. According to Commissioner Harry Anslinger of the Federal Bureau of Narcotics, there are approximately fifty to sixty thousand illegal users in this country. Other authorities have called this figure preposterous. A 1954 report to the Attorney General of California, for instance, stated that there were ten thousand illegal users named in the state criminal files. "But," it continued, "this is assumed to be less than half the true figure." If there are twenty thousand addicts in California alone, Mr. Anslinger's figure of thirty to forty thousand in the rest of the country becomes, to say the least, questionable. But, let us accept it nevertheless. It is still obvious that three institutions of limited capacity can accommodate only a small fraction of the drug-addict population.

The population at Lexington and Fort Worth consists of addicts who have voluntarily committed themselves for treatment and federal prisoner addicts who are committed to serve their sentences there. Most patients leave these institutions in thirty days or less. But, what of those who stay for a longer period of time? Is a permanent rehabilitation likely to result? Judge Morris Ploscowe in a recent report prepared for the use of the Joint Committee of the American Bar Association and the American Medical Association on Narcotic Drugs stated that the likelihood of a cure at one of these institutions is remote. He said:

The programs of the institutions like Lexington, Fort Worth and Riverside are directed towards: (1) successfully withdrawing the patients from drugs; (2) building them up physically; (3) strengthening their vocational skills so that they can become productive members of the community; (4) eliminating gaps in their educational backgrounds; (5) attempting to give them understanding as to why they have had to resort to drugs in order to cope with life's problems; and (6) enabling them to resist the compulsion to use drugs as a means of resolving their difficulties.

There can be no doubt that institutions like Lexington, Fort Worth and Riverside have been a great deal more successful in the first four aspects of their programs than in giving addicts a thorough understanding of why they use drugs and a resolve to resist the compulsion of drugs in the future. Addicts undoubtedly benefit considerably from their stays in Lexington. Fort Worth, and Riverside. Their systems are cleared of drugs, they become physically healthier and stronger. They are taught habits of regular work and may learn some academic subjects. *But the exposure to a few months of a minimum amount of psychiatry, social casework educational and vocational activity, cannot eradicate the deep-seated necessity and compulsion for drugs which most addicts seem to have. There are no magic cures at narcotics hospitals. We simply do not know enough about the processes of drug addiction to produce such cures.*

The statistics on relapse to addiction after attempted cures at narcotics hospitals like Lexington, Fort Worth or Riverside, tells the stark story of the basic failure of the hospital-centered approach in dealing with problems of drug addiction. (Italics ours)

Now, what cure was the Eighty-fourth Congress talking about? If our hospital facilities are woefully limited and their therapy completely inadequate and if doctors are forbidden to treat addicts, where can an addict go to get a cure? There is no place.

And so, in desperation, some addicts who have found a degree of freedom from their addiction, have banded together to help themselves stay off drugs by helping other addicts. They call themselves Narcotics Anonymous, and utilize the program and methods of Alcoholics Anonymous. Narcotics Anonymous or N.A., as it is known, has only one condition for membership: an applicant must have an honest desire to get off the habit. Doubtless, N. A. can offer the addict something he cannot obtain anywhere else, a deep understanding that comes from identification. Also, in N.A., an addict can feel that he is not criminal or contemptible, and that he does not stand alone. For instance, when a shamefaced new member admits that he has pawned his mother's jewelry to get the drugs, an old-timer tells how he had pilfered his wife's purse.

A new member tells that he forged drug prescriptions, and his sponsor, now off drugs, says that he almost murdered a hospital attendant to get into the drug closet. The N.A. member first shares his own shame with newcomers and then his hope for them as well as himself.

Like A.A., N.A. believes that a person must take twelve "steps" before he can hope to stay away from drugs permanently. He is not driven toward the steps but takes them as he feels willing and able. The steps, as old members know them, are:

1. We admitted that we were powerless over drugs—that our lives had become unmanageable.
2. Came to believe that a Power greater than ourselves could restore us to sanity.
3. Made a decision to turn our will and our lives over to the care of God as we understood Him.
4. Made a searching and fearless moral inventory of ourselves.

5. Admitted to God, to ourselves and to another human being the exact nature of our wrongs.
6. Were entirely ready to have God remove all these defects of character.
7. Humbly asked Him to remove our shortcomings.
8. Made a list of all persons we had harmed, and became willing to make amends to them all.
9. Made direct amends to such people wherever possible, except when to do so would injure them or others.
10. Continued to take personal inventory and when we were wrong, promptly admitted it.
11. Sought through prayer and meditation to improve our conscious contact with God as we understood Him, praying only for knowledge of His will for us and the power to carry that out.
12. Having had a spiritual awakening as the result of these steps, we tried to carry this message to other addicts and practice these principles in all our affairs.

The most important step is the twelfth, for that is the one that symbolizes the warmth and friendliness of human beings for one another, according to members of N.A.

Unfortunately, Narcotics Anonymous has not been nearly as effective as Alcoholics Anonymous. While Alcoholics Anonymous has a large membership and maintains groups throughout the country, Narcotics Anonymous has only four groups—in Lexington, Kentucky, in New York City, in Washington, D.C., and in Santa Monica, California. While Alcoholics Anonymous can point to thousands of "cures," Narcotics Anonymous admits that for all its hard work and good intentions, it has been influential in effecting only a very few recoveries.

Why is this? First, perhaps because of the public attitude toward addiction. After all, an A.A. member, on an errand of mercy to a sick or backsliding alcoholic, can give him a drink to stave off the shakes or delirium while he talks to him —while if the N.A. member gave a sick addict the shot he needed, he might find himself facing a long jail term. Actually, however, when one tries to account for the basic failure of N.A., he must recognize that the addict's own personality is the chief reason. The addict, unlike the alcoholic, has no urge for gregariousness. He takes his drug because he needs to retire into a dream-world of his own. He seeks aloneness while the alcoholic looks for companionship. Therefore, the friendliness inherent in the cures of both A.A. and N.A., while it makes a big difference to the alcoholic, must leave most addicts untouched. Addicts, tragically, have still to learn the *need* for friendship.

Is there, then, an answer for the addict? The answer, as illustrated by the experiences of other countries, is definitely *yes*. In England, for example, there are less than four hundred known drug addicts. In England, however, the words *criminal addict* are never heard. And doctors are allowed to dispense drugs to users and to treat them either in their own offices or in clinics. We should follow England's example and require the Treasury Department to conform its policy with the law of our land as set forth by our Supreme Court. An addict is a sick person. His addiction is a symptom of a complex pathology. If a doctor feels that drugs should be administered in limited quantities, either temporarily or indefinitely in the course of treating this pathological condition, he should not be interfered with by the threat of penal sanctions. At present, dope addiction and the pathological conditions underlying it constitute the only maladies for which a patient may not receive treatment from his physician in accordance with the doctor's own best medical judgment.

However, the problem of American addiction, thanks in large measure to the policy of the Treasury Department, has become so acute that we must go beyond mere permissiveness toward the medical profession and evolve more aggressive methods for coping with this illness. For this reason many experts have suggested that we set up narcotics clinics which would attempt to cure addicts, and, at the same time, dispense free or low-cost drugs to those who cannot do without them. But the Treasury Department, despite its dismal failure at controlling the drug traffic in other ways, is opposed to any experiment that includes legal dispensation. Commissioner Harry J. Anslinger labels the idea of legalized clinics "nonsense." He relies on so-called tradition to bolster his case. He says, "Legalized clinics cannot work in this country. They never have worked since they were first opened in 1919."

Interestingly, during 1919 and for some years before that, the Treasury Department, despite its actions, revealed a certain sympathy for the addict and deplored the fact that the law forced them into criminal activity. The Department's 1919 report encouraged local health departments to set up clinics where addicts could receive carefully regulated amounts of drugs and be encouraged at the same time to overcome their habits. Such clinics were established in forty-odd cities. Some of them appeared to be fairly successful, although many took insufficient precautions to assure that addicts would not obtain drugs from more than one source or failed to ascertain that they were treating actual addicts, so that sometimes peddlers came and sold the drugs they received from the clinics.

Because of these abuses, and without either an attempt to improve the administration of the clinics or to make an honest evaluation of their validity, the Treasury Department decided in 1924 to close all the clinics. Even those which had been extolled by medical authorities and police officers alike—the ones in Shreveport, Louisiana, and Los Angeles, California—were shut. When asked for an explanation, the Department merely stated that it was opposed to treatment of addicts that involved administering drugs.

Today, the Treasury Department stands on its 1924 position. It cites the administrative failures of those early clinics, unreviewed and basically unimportant by comparison to the larger issue, as justification for its negative attitude. Unfortunately, the Department has potent allies. A recent report of a U.S. Senate subcommittee stated:

"The subcommittee is unalterably opposed to and rejects the clinic plan proposed for supplying narcotics addicts with free or low cost drugs. We are opposed to all types of so-called ambulatory treatment.... Finally, we believe the thought of permanently maintaining drug addiction with 'sustaining' doses of narcotics drugs to be utterly repugnant to the moral principles inherent in our law and the character of our people."

What in "the moral principles inherent in our law" dictates that we should deny drugs to one who cannot resist them because of a psychological craving or compulsion? Is there really anything in the moral law that suggests that we cannot ease the misery and suffering of an addict by the temporary, or if medically indicated, the continued administration of limited quantities of drugs? Indeed is it not rather a violation of the moral law to deny the addict the solace and comfort of the medical practitioner and thereby to drive him into the hands of the underworld?

There are those who say addicts cannot be rehabilitated. But how do they know? It is certainly obvious that nobody knows very much about addicts and their needs. Who can tell whether or not the clinics can help pull them out of the trap in which they are caught?

Over the years, numerous proposals for clinics have been advanced by conservative physicians, medical societies, lawyers and responsible community groups. And after considering all of their worthwhile plans, we offer a practical solution that may be even more workable.

Narcotic hospital facilities under federal auspices could be established in all large cities. These would institutionalize addicts for a period of at least two months, during which time they would be withdrawn from narcotics and exposed to a rehabilitative program, including contact with doctors, psychiatrists, social workers, vocational and recreational guidance personnel, etc.

After their release from the hospital, addicts would become outpatients in the clinical attachment of their hospitals. Efforts at rehabilitation would be continued, with the addicts receiving medical, psychiatric and social service. Those whose hospital withdrawals were successful would be treated without drugs; those who reverted after leaving the hospital and were proved to be in need of drugs, would get at cost the amounts their doctors prescribed for them. Gradual withdrawal would be re-attempted with them when their psychiatrists judged the supportive therapy to have taken sufficient hold so that they could rely on it instead of the drug. Those who were considered "incurable" by the clinic professionals would be released from therapy while still receiving indicated dosages of their drug.

Drugs would be given addicts for self-administration, but no more than two days' supply would be furnished at any one time. There would also be safeguards against addicts registering in more than one clinic. These would include fingerprinting and photographing. As for the current police machinery, it could be used almost entirely and far more effectively than at present for suppression of the illicit market.

Clinics could serve as research centers on addiction. Certainly, we need to have a great many questions answered before we can hope to launch a fundamental attack on addiction. Can drug users be restored outside institutional walls? Can supportive therapy help them face the stresses of daily living without resort to drugs? After all, the test of rehabilitation is not whether an addict can exist without drugs in an institution, but whether he can function without them in the community. As for the unrehabilitable addicts, can they be transformed into productive people if their drug needs are met? It is time we found out the answers to these questions.

Of course, treating addicts in hospitals and clinics will cost money. But, when we consider that an ever-increasing percentage of those in our jails and reformatories are addicted, and bound to be jailed again and again until they die, we must see the financial practicality of a clinic plan. More importantly, the clinic plan can turn some sick parasites into productive people. And it can put the skids under the billion-dollar narcotics racketeers who are giving this country a bad reputation throughout the world. If we manage to take the profit out of contraband drugs, the mobsters will doubtless stop trying to create new drug markets for themselves. Actually, when we consider the whole picture of gangsterdom and addiction, a program of legalized clinics is the most effective way yet evolved for delivering our children from the "drug menace."

Chapter **3** **So Long as They Have Life**

Unfortunately, our Congress refuses to consider the tie-up between gangsterdom and addiction. It has accepted the word of our Commissioner of Narcotics and has ignored the advice of knowledgeable doctors, psychiatrists, educators, social workers and lawyers. It is blind to the true problem. Perhaps its eyes will be opened if the people speak out. Congressional awareness, which we must work to achieve, can bring about the establishment of clinics and do away with punishment and incarceration for addicts.

How do we achieve Congressional awareness? There are many ways. We can encourage our state Legislative Commissions on Youth and Delinquency to hold public hearings at which experts from the medical societies, bar associations, welfare councils and social agencies would testify. Such hearings could start a process whereby changes in our federal and our state laws would be demanded and made. County and state committees on drug addiction, consisting of both professional and interested lay people, should be established to study the problem and seek reform. Besides, interested individuals should state their views to their legislators and congressmen and work for a complete change in federal policy—a policy that since 1930 has been advanced and promoted by Commissioner Harry J. Anslinger, who stands

143

today as the most potent obstacle to the adoption of the clinic plan, and does not hesitate to express his opposition.

"From time to time," the Commissioner stated in the January, 1959, issue of the F.B.I. *Law Enforcement Bulletin,* "certain individuals who consider themselves 'experts' have publicized their answer to the narcotic problem. They say it is simple. All you have to do is to take the profit out of the traffic, and the problem is solved. When asked how you take the profit out, they say that is also simple—just give the addicts all they want for nothing.

"The plan is so simple that only a simpleton could think it up."

Simpleton? Now to which simpleton could the Commissioner be referring? To the eminent late Dr. Hubert Howe who pioneered for clinics for addicts? To the equally eminent Drs. Lawrence Kolb, Herbert Berger and Andrew E. Eggston who are pioneering today? To simpletons like Judge Jonah Goldstein, Judge Morris Ploscowe, Colonel Harold Riegelman? Simpletons like the New York Academy of Medicine, the Committee on Public Health of the New York State Bar Association, the Richmond County Medical Society, the Citizens Advisory Committee to the Attorney General of California?

Commissioner Anslinger continues in the *Bulletin,* "The adoption of such a plan [clinic] as advocated by . . . dewy-eyed, impractical, self-styled social reformers would lead only to disaster. Their championing of the drug addict, an immoral vicious social leper, is another example of the many wild schemes advanced by certain theorists outside law enforcement. They ignore the whole concept of American justice—that man is responsible for his actions and that the wrongdoer should be punished by swift and impartial justice."

Now what justice could Commissioner Anslinger be thinking of—American justice or storm troppers' justice? American justice is not cavalier. It is not heavy-booted. American justice tries to understand the malignancy of the misfit. American justice accepts the assistance of the sciences—psychiatry, medicine, sociology and theology. American justice rejects the idea that all deviates are cattle to be stamped and tagged and branded—and punished. American justice, thank God, takes some account of the notion of charity as Christ preached it.

Christian charity? Well, Commissioner Anslinger recoils, shivering, at what might happen if those who believe in it have their way. With a heroic spirit he predicts a dark, dreary future if America follows the line of thinking of the clinic plan advocates to what he calls "a logical conclusion." He says that "then there would be no objection to the state setting aside a building where on the first floor there would be a bar for alcoholics, on the second floor licensed prostitutes, with the third floor set aside for sexual deviates, and crowning them all, on the top floor a drug-dispensing station for addicts. All services would be subsidized by the state."

What un-Godly, unfriendly words. What shoddy humor. And how strange to hear a man in the Commissioner's position speaking with so little restraint. Should not a responsible public servant have greater balance? Commissioner Anslinger's wit reveals all too clearly his hostility and his prejudice.

Here is a man who has been assigned the important job of cleansing America of addiction. How can we hope that he will accomplish that job when addicts, the people with whom he ought to be concerned, are no more to him than "immoral vicious social lepers"?

How can Commissioner Anslinger clean up addiction if he does not approach the addict's problems sympathetically? And would he, the high mogul of our narcotics program, ever "stoop" to search an addict's soul? If he did, he might conceive new techniques for controlling addiction. If he did, he could not fight the clinic plan for combatting addiction.

But Commissioner Anslinger would never "stoop." He is inaccessible and intolerant to the demands and pleas of the community for a change of policy. And our Congress is satisfying his thirst for vengeance and instinct for hate against the addict. It is a wonder that after thirty years in his job our government still permits Commissioner Anslinger to continue to formulate its policy toward addicts.

There is only one way to start reform—retire Commissioner Anslinger and replace him with a distinguished public health administrator of vision and perception and, above all, heart. Such a man would not fight against clinics; he would be bound to fight *for* them.

Of course, so long as our national policy remains static, drug addicts will continue to create a serious situation in all our communities. Therefore, we must, ourselves, take constructive action to counteract the problems in our own areas. We ought to see to it that ways and means are developed in our communities for helping present addicts and preventing the creation of new ones. Through our social agencies, churches, P.-T.A.'s, Leagues of Women Voters, and men's service clubs such as Kiwanis and Rotary, we ought to assess our problems, particularly as they relate to teen-agers. How many teen-age users are there in our communities? How many pushers that the authorities know about? How many teen-agers have come to the attention of the courts? How many to the attention of the voluntary agencies? What about our community law enforcement, legislation, education? What about the quality and quantity of mental-hygiene services available in our communities? How do our policemen feel about addicts, and what is our teachers' attitude? What programs against addiction are being carried on in our schools, churches and other organizations?

Let us start with our churches. Many experts believe that the church has a superb opportunity to reach addicts, but that it has thus far failed to do so.

According to the Reverend Doctor Bridgeman, Chairman of Bishop Donegan's Special Committee on the Problems of Narcotics of the Episcopal Diocese of New York, present addicts, while not active members of any church, were church-goers in their youth. "From this," he says, "we learn that the church has failed to help these people at a time when they needed help and also that when our clergy say 'we have no addicts in our congregations,' it can be no consolation to us because we know that addicts break with the church. It is our duty to seek out these lost sheep and to help them."

How can the church help young addicts? First it can accept them, not shun them, as so many other agencies do. It can work with parents to make them know that addiction is a disease, not a crime. It can see to it that its young peoples' groups offer addicts who are attempting to kick their habits encouragement and normal social associations. More important, it can make addicts aware of potentialities in themselves that are worth living and fighting for.

"Bringing out the potentialities of some addicts," the Reverend Doctor Bridgeman says, "may consist of encouragement of a traditional sort of religious experience, either because it has emotional power, in that it stirs old memories, or because it is a brand-new idea and a fresh approach."

But most addicts cannot ordinarily be reached through religion in their early contacts with the church. They claim to be atheists or agnostics, and only come to church in the first place because clergymen and counselors reveal warmth toward them. And yet, despite addicts' general lack of religion, some members of the clergy report great satisfaction in their contacts with them. The hands that are held out to addicts are so few that they become dependent on any that are. Thus, some addicts who begin coming to church out of no more than their need for the comradeship may eventually acquire faith and belief.

As noteworthy as rehabilitation for individual addicts is, our churches can do an even more important job when it comes to the matter of arousing intelligent public opinion in favor of legislation that can help addicts out of their misery. Certainly, our churches believe in humane benevolence, not vengeance, toward all sick people, including addicts. They should let the authorities know their views. Perhaps through the churches, more than through any other medium, our authorities will perceive the errors in their policies toward addiction.

It is said by many experts that the school is in an even better position than the church to combat addiction, but Commissioner Anslinger has fought education against addiction as violently as he has fought clinics for addicts. He says that education defeats its purpose, that some youngsters might be induced to try narcotics if they hear about them and that academic discussion is useless with addicts or potential addicts. Most educators regard Anslinger's position as ridiculous. One of the many Anslinger critics is Dr. Clare C. Baldwin, Assistant Superintendent of the New York City public schools. He says:

". . . I would be the first one to drop the discussion of the dangers of narcotics addiction from our educational program if I had any assurance that the problem or the danger did not threaten. I think nothing is more wasteful than a purely academic discussion of a problem. If we took this to some remote island where there was no possibility that there would be any drugs in the community, I think we should be as silly as if we were discussing how many angels could dance on the point of a needle, but the point on which Anslinger and I clash directly is the question of whether or not it is academic to discuss the danger of narcotics addiction with children who are immediately exposed to the problem. For him to tell me that there is no problem in New York City, and that we should not discuss it because we might encourage some kid to try it, is about the silliest viewpoint on education I ever heard. When you have fifty of them in a junior high school who are already trying it and who tell you they don't know anything about it and they are hungry to be told what is the trouble here, somebody has to break the vacuum. It is not an academic discussion, notwithstanding Mr. Anslinger, who said nobody who used drugs was in school. So for us to talk about whether we are going to educate or not is not a question that even needs discussion. It is a question of how soon are you going to do it and what are you going to tell them?

". . . A presentation of the dangers of narcotics use is not academic in Boston or Washington or Philadelphia or Los Angeles or Pittsburgh or any other large city. It is certainly not academic here in New York."

Psychiatrist Dr. James Toolan backs Dr. Baldwin's view. He says, "There is no indication that one single youngster has become addicted just because of the educational processes, and I think that we should look upon this in the same way we look upon venereal-disease education. The same hullabaloo was raised twenty-five years ago. You read reports in the literature which indicated that if you talked about venereal disease and gave sex education, every youngster in the country would go out to have sexual intercourse. I think venereal-disease education is an accepted procedure. I don't think that what has been proclaimed has happened. It is not what is taught, but how. You can give the best advice in the world and cause evil by it. It depends on how it is put over. If handled by properly trained teachers, social workers, whoever is interested in the problem, it can be good. I personally was shocked when the Commissioner of Narcotics in this country objected to the educational resources being brought to bear on the problem."

The New York City school system, despite Treasury Department pressure, has had an educational program for several years for both its teachers and its students. Although the New York Board of Education is the first to recognize that youngsters with defective personality structures who are looking for relief from their inner tensions will not be deterred from narcotics by education, it says that its program does combat the tendency to experimentation by which some adolescents slide into addiction. And when a child is an addict, it says, teacher education, giving teachers an awareness of the problem, enables them to spot and possibly to help him.

Probably the most important phase of the New York City program is its teacher training. When the Board first began training teachers it found that the whole field of addiction was new to them. Many New York teachers did not know that "reefers" meant marijuana cigarettes. They did not know that "horse" meant heroin. They did not know what youngsters meant when they talked about "being on the mainline."

"When we first began our teacher-training program," Dr. Baldwin says, "we did not have much to work on. We had a little bulletin we threw together very quickly on which the Police Department helped. We called together all the community leaders and the principals of schools, and a Police Department representative discussed with us this whole subject of drug addiction. He had with him his demonstration kit. I don't think it was accidental that immediately after that, or within a matter of weeks, we had a great rise in the number of adolescent drug cases that we had identified, simply because these people went back and interpreted the problem to the teachers. They began to look for bent spoons; they began to identify syringes that they found in lavatories. They began to see the physical symptoms. They looked for signs that they knew nothing about before. At one time, a few years ago, we had forty-seven identified cases in one junior high school."

Identified cases of addiction in the New York City public schools are handled not by policemen but by guidance counselors who work closely with children and parents, as well as with community agencies, psychiatric, religious and social.

The schools also give group guidance lessons on the evils of addiction. They use all kinds of educational devices, including recording and films. The best of the films they use is one released by *Encyclopaedia Britannica* called "Drug Addiction." It is an honest portrayal, frightening in its starkness, but never sensational. In addition to the lectures and the media presentation, New York schools stimulate their children to create posters and write essays. One of the posters done by a seventh grader some years ago and used today reads, "Don't be a dope, addict." And a few examples of the essays written by seventh and eighth graders follow because they seem such eloquent arguments for education:

One boy wrote: "While I was in the eighth grade my guidance teacher told our class of the dangers of narcotics. We have learned that it will become a habit that cannot be stopped by yourself. In my block there is a house where the addicts and peddlers hang out. Every day I see people who use the stuff. I even see people who cannot afford it, how they suffer from lack of heroin or cocaine. Many girls prostitute just so they can get money for dope. This happens every day around my block and neighborhood.

"I remember just before my summer vacation there were five boys that robbed, stole and everything else just to get dope. Then they got caught and sent away. They came back cured, but they went right back to the use of dope."

Another boy, in the seventh grade, wrote: "What I have learned about narcotics: I have learned that I should not hang around any person who uses dope or narcotics. But I have run into such cases such as being with boys who use narcotics. While I was going home one night a man asked me would I like something fine. I didn't stop because I knew what he meant. Because a boy told me someone stopped him. So I seventh grade, a teacher found him mainlining in the boys' full of narcotics, and told me to hold it. So because I didn't hold it or take one he called me a name. But that did not hurt me.

"My suggestion about the narcotics problem is to try to tell those boys what they are up against. But if it wasn't for the school I would have been in that racket, too. That is what I learned about narcotics. And from the school."

There is no question but that the New York school program

fortifies children somewhat against the approaches, insinua-
tions and threats of the peddlers. It also makes an attempt,
and sometimes a most effective one, to deal with their personal
problems. And so, the schools sometimes have significant
success in reaching young addicts.

Martin Roberts is one among several such cases. He was
a seclusive, withdrawn Harlem boy. Not being obstreperous
as many delinquent types are, he was generally ignored by
teachers and classmates alike. When he was thirteen and in
seventh grade, a teacher found him mainlining in the boys'
room. He immediately referred Martin to the school guidance
counselor, who discovered that he had been joy-popping for
about a year. The counselor went to see Martin's family.

"I thought I was pretty shockproof," she said, "but I was
horrified at the way that family lived. Nine of them in two
small, dark, rat-infested rooms. The father had left the home
a couple of years before and the mother was confined to bed
with a heart condition. The household was being supported by
Martin's two older brothers who resented every bite the littler
children put in their mouths. Martin's sister, sixteen and not
quite bright, was in full charge of the home. She too had hard
feelings toward the younger children, including Martin, because she felt they tied her down.

"Martin was a sensitive child and he naturally blamed
himself because the older brothers and sister disliked him.
Almost as soon as I met him, I knew he was hungry for love
and affection."

After her visit to Martin's home, the guidance counselor
contacted the Community Service Society, which began working with the family. First, the family was moved out of their
deplorable quarters and into a housing project. For the first
time in Martin's young life, he knew what it was to have
enough room. The Society then arranged for supplementary
relief so that some of the pressure could be off Martin's
brothers. They also offered the family outside housekeeping
service so that Martin's sister would have time to attend a
vocational school. Martin himself was given a case worker
who showed a vital interest in everything that concerned him,
and a "big brother." Every Saturday, his big brother took him
out. They went to movies, to baseball games, to the Aquarium,

to the Museum of Natural History. During the summer, they took outings into the country.

"Martin became very attached to his big brother," the guidance counselor says. "I believe his big brother had a great deal to do with his giving up the habit. Oh yes, he's been off for four years now. He's in high school and doing well. Every once in a while, he comes back to see me and our principal. He likes to boast to us about being 'clean.' He says that nowadays he is acting like a teacher himself. He says, 'I tell other kids I meet what fools they are to try junk and ket hooked. I teach them everything I learned about junk while I was going to this school.'

"It's a thrill to us when Martin comes back to see us. It makes us feel our work is worth while."

Martin Roberts proves how wrong Commissioner Anslinger and our Congress are. Who can say—certainly not they—what addicts to whom we extend understanding, love, and affection will be doing tomorrow? Addicts are like all people. They can change so long as they have life.

The terms included here are not limited to drug-addiction argot but represent also other phases of the secret language of the underworld, the special lingos of the prostitution racket, prison slang, and police journalese: all as they impinge upon and overlap each other. Many of them have other special meanings in other special argots; but the definitions given here represent their usage in this book. This mere handful of terms, out of the thousands which exist in the protective code of the underworld, typify the color, imagination, and subtlety with which the hunted evade detectives, outwit eavesdroppers, and confound tourists and other squares.

This glossary was prepared by Maria Leach, student of American dialects, folk speech, and slang, and member of the American Dialect Society.

alky A person addicted to alcohol; an alcoholic.

Bams Weak marijuana cigarettes.
banana 1. Sexual intercourse. 2. A police informant.
bird An informer; a stool piegon; one who will *sing*.
bit A jail sentence; a term in prison. —**long bit** A long term in prison.
blow (one's) lump To give full expression to one's emotions.
book Same as *paper*.
boot A thrill; a kick; especially, the exhilaration from a narcotic drug. —**to go on the boot** To leave the needle in the arm after the drug is absorbed, to twitch it and bring on bleeding and pain: a masochistic practice for experiencing an added boot.
boot-and-shoer An ineffectual, penniless, down-and-out addict, especially one who begs his shots by threatening to inform.
bread Money. —**front the bread** Show the money. —**pass the bread** Pay the money.
bugged up Aware; in the know; also, angry, in an ugly frame of mind.

153

burn To reveal a stool pigeon as such to other addicts, peddlers, pushers, etc.

bust An arrest: by extension from earlier drug-addiction lingo
in which a **bust** is a police raid on a drug-users' hangout.
—busted Arrested.

cap Abbreviation for *capsule*: the standard dose of a drug.

cat A fellow; a regular guy: not a *square;* also, a swing
musician, a hepcat.

chick A young girl; any woman. **—fly chick** A prostitute.
—working chick A prostitute.

clean Not using, needing, or craving a drug; not drugged; not
addicted.

chirp To inform; to sing; by extension from *bird*.

connection A seller of narcotics to users; the person from whom
an addict buys his *stuff*.

cool Very much all right; fitting and proper; up to date; hep.

cop To name, identify, or reveal to the police.

crack Talk, especially sarcastic or misleading talk. **—no crack**
No kidding.

deuce Two dollars.

dig To see; look at; hear; listen to; love; understand; appreciate.
—plant you now and dig you later Leave you now and see
you later.

dommy A place to live; domicile.

down Depressed; worried.

dropped Arrested; picked up by the cops.

drug, drug out Depressed; tired.

Dynamiters Extra-strong reefers.

Fed A federal agent; especially, an agent of the Federal Bureau
of Narcotics.

finger To name, identify, or reveal to the police.

fix To give a ration or a shot of a narcotic drug to; also, the
ration or the shot of the drug.

fly right To think clearly and behave correctly.

gang shag A sex session of a gang.

gazer A federal agent in search of narcotics.

gees Guys. *Ghees* is the more usual spelling of this term: so pronounced.

get gone To become or feel exhilarated; to feel out of this world.

get sent To feel or become exhilarated, especially from music, alcohol, or a drug.

gimpies The police; a mocking term for any people beneath one's notice; also jerks; cripples who cannot walk upright.

glim To see; look at; sometimes, to know.

goof A pusher's customer: a term of contempt used by non-addicted pushers.

on the goof Drowsy, dreamy, relaxed; under the influence of a narcotic drug; on the nod. See *high*.

griefer Same as *boot-and-shoer*.

in the groove Doing superbly: by extension from the swing-music usage meaning "playing in exalted mood and perfectly."

the habit Dependence on drugs: drug addiction. —**to kick the habit** To break the drug habit; to stop using narcotics.

hack A prison guard.

handkerchief-head An unenlightened, behind-the-times Negro from the South.

headshrinker A psychiatrist.

hincty Stuck up, snooty, snobbish: a Negro term that originated in the early Harlem night spots.

high 1. Exhilarated or intoxicated by marijuana or some other narcotic drug. 2. Drowsy, dreamy, relaxed, especially from opium or an opiate.

hip Clever smart; wise; sophisticated; in the know.

hipster One who is *hip*.

hood A racketeer: contraction of hoodlum.

hooked Completely addicated to a drug; so addicted as to suffer agony without it.

hop Opium; in loose usage, narcotic drugs in general.

hophead An opium addict.

horse Heroin.

hot shot A fatal bullet.

jive The jargon or special language of swing music and swing musicians plus New York Negro slang, plus drug-addiction argot: a secret and special lingo incomprehensible to the *squares;* hence, confusing, meaningless, or misleading language. By extension *jive* has come to mean kidding, insincere talk. —**junkie jive** Specifically, drug-addiction argot.

joy-pop A subcutaneous injection of a drug. Drug-induced exhilaration has been called *joy* since the 1920s. The term **joy-poppers** is often applied to a beginner in drug using or to one who uses drugs only intermittently.

jump stink To turn hostile; to let (a person) down.

junk A narcotic drug; also, narcotic drugs in general.

junker 1. A drug addict. 2. A drug peddler. —**social junkers** Gang members who get together at specified times to take shots together for kicks and prestige; not habitual users.

junkie 1. A drug addict: a more usual term than *junker*. 2. A drug peddler.

junk hog A drug addict; a junkie who has excessive demand for narcotics.

kick 1. The wonderful feeling, thrill, satisfaction, or reaction resulting from a dose of a narcotic drug. 2. The drug itself.

kite A message from one prison inmate to another. —**while the kite flew** While the message traveled from cell to cell.

lay down cold on To betray; to let down.

long-tailed rat An informer; a stool pigeon of the lowest order.

mainline 1. The median cephalic vein in the forearm into which some drug users inject the narcotic drug. 2. The intravenous injection itself.

mainliner A drug addict who habitually takes his drug by intravenous injection.

midget A child so small or young as to be nonsuspect as a go-between between a drug user and a seller.

mob An organized group active in the same racket: sometimes a neighborhood gang, sometimes of national proportions.

to have a monkey on (one's) back To experience the distress and symptoms of drug withdrawal.

mouse A stool pigeon.

mug 1. A stupid person; a fool. 2. In some usages, anyone not belonging to the underworld.

nod Sleep. —**on the nod** Sleepy or stuporous from an opiate.

oil-burning habit The drug habit.

okey-doke Jail: perhaps a rhyming-slang formation from *pokey*, which means county jail.

omerta The tradition and code of secrecy and loyalty of the Mafia. Any violation of omerta is punished by death.

paper A very thin paper fold containing a small amount of a drug: also called *book, card, deck.*

pipes Opium smokers; opium addicts.

plant Any secret place where illegal goods are stored; also, the goods stored; specifically, the place where a drug importer or dealer stashes the narcotics.

plant manager The administrator of the plant, supervisor of the subplants where the stuff is cut and packaged, director of the runners, etc.

pot Marijuana.

pounder The cop on the beat.

punk An underling in a gang or mob.

pusher One who peddles or sells narcotic drugs.

put that mess down Tell that story.

rat An informer; a stool pigeon.

reefer A marijuana cigarette.

right man The top drug importer of a specific mob.

rinkey-dink Ancient and broken down.

rooster The buttocks.

Rover Boys The cops.

rumble A real gang fight.

runner One who delivers the cut and packaged narcotics to wholesalers.

salt and pepper Marijuana: said also of any other essential drug.

salty Unfriendly; hostile.

score Enough money to buy narcotics. —**to score** To buy drugs from a pusher or a connection; to pay a pusher or a connection.

screw A prison guard.

scumpteen Very much of.

shooting gallery 1. Any specific place where drug users meet (or go) to take their shots or injections. Among teenagers this is often the unfrequented hallway or cellar of a tenement. 2. In the U.S. Public Health Service Hospital, Lexington, Kentucky, the withdrawal ward.

sing   To inform; to betray (one's associates).

skid row   In the U.S. Public Health Service Hospital, Lexington, Kentucky, the convalescent ward.

skin-pop   To inject a drug under the skin: distinguished from injecting it intravenously.

skullbust   To give much information to.

snap (one's) cap   To talk fast.

sniff   To inhale powdered heroin or cocaine.

snort   Same as *sniff*.

snow   Cocaine.

solid   Good; solid as the rock of Gibraltar.

special employee   A stool pigeon.

speedball   A shot containing heroin, cocaine, and marijuana (sometimes only heroin and cocaine).

square   One who lives according to the conventional social and moral code; specifically, a nonaddict; one who knows nothing about drug addiction; anyone not in the know.

squealer   An informer: one who betrays his associates.

stable   A pimp's group of girls.

stash-sitter   The resident guardian of a plant.

stoned   Unconscious and insensate from a drug.

stone-hitter   A muscle man of a gang or mob.

stool, stoolie   A stool pigeon.

stuff   Narcotics in general.

sweet man   A prostitute's pimp.

take off   To get high.

tea   Marijuana. —**to sip tea**   To smoke marijuana.

trick   A prostitute's customer.

trilly   To walk in a light carefree manner.

uncles   Federal agents.

vibrating   In the groove.

vigorish   Money; payment.

viper   A marijuana (or opium) addict.

walk To be released from legal custody; to go free.

weed Marijuana.

whiskers Federal officers; T-men.

the works The outfit needed for taking narcotics hypodermically: a hypodermic syringe and needle and a piece of cotton, or their homemade substitutes (eye dropper, needle or safety pin, and a bent spoon).

yard-dog A lowly but extremely loyal attaché.

yen The unendurable craving of a drug addict deprived of his drug. The term *yenyen* originally meant a craving for opium.

N.B.: Much that appears in this book is essentially a fictionalized version of events that have occurred and are occurring in centers of drug traffic throughout the United States. Some of the leading figures are referred to by their true names; others are composites of characters well known in police circles.